RHYTHM

SAVING ABBIE BOOK 5

MAGGIE ALABASTER

Before I Stay
    Written by Landon Flynn

You want to give me all of your soul,
    But your eye is on the door.
    Your hand is on the handle, ready to turn,
    But you step toward me.

You want to step beside me,
    But you're standing very still.
    You need to jump with your eyes open,
    But you close them anyway.

You know exactly what I need,
    Because you need it too.
    You know the words you want to say,
    But they won't come before you go.

You're lying here beside me,
    But you're never really here.
    You need to stop and hold me,
    Before I stay.
    Before I stay.

Come and walk beside me,

So we can both stay.

Can both stay.

Can both stay.

1

ABBIE

"Yes, I realise that." Jackson ran a hand over his head and curled his fingers into his hair in frustration. He looked like he was ready to throw his phone across the hotel room.

"If it's just… Then why do they…" He listened and threw his hand up in the air. "Okay, I get that, but I need my lead guitarist for the sound check in the morning."

I sighed and leaned back against Asher's chest. The drummer slid his arms around me and nestled his face into my hair.

"It'll be okay," he said softly. "Jackson and Levi will get it sorted out."

"Yeah, I know." I had to believe that. The band's manager had been on the phone with the Dublin police, the Perth police and fuck knows who else for hours. By the sound of it, he was going around in circles. No wonder he looked pissed now.

"I can't stop picturing Tully getting into the back of that police car." I saw it over and over in my head on continuous repeat. My heart ached each time.

The guitarist had looked calm and composed as always, but he must have been a nervous wreck on the inside.

I was.

The police hadn't said he was under arrest, just that he needed to answer some questions about the death of his adopted father. If the authorities had an inkling Tully was the one who killed him, surely they knew it was in self-defence? Xavier Lang pulled a gun on him and would have killed Tully to prove his loyalty to Dante Fiorelli. That was some fucked up shit right there.

Almost as fucked up as Zeke's evil twin brothers, Hunter and Parker, helping clean up the mess of dead bodies left behind us. Right before they assaulted Penn.

Tully left Australia with us immediately after Xavier Lang's death. The police might consider that an admission of guilt.

"He'll be fine," Asher assured me. "They'll explore

all the legal channels, then the illegal ones. Whatever it takes."

"If anyone can talk their way out of it, it's Tully," Zeke said. The lead singer of Wolf Venom looked a lot more chill than I felt. He usually did. Right now, he was leaning back against the wall, arms crossed, one eye on Jackson and the other on me. How could he look so fucking calm? Especially when it was a façade. He was on alert for anything, always. That was what came from growing up in a family whose business was organised crime.

"And if he can't talk his way out of it?" I put my hands on Asher's arms to cuddle him tighter. Assurances were nice, but I needed the comfort of physical contact. His hard, muscular body certainly gave me that.

"Then we start calling in favours," Zeke said with a shrug. "Or doing a few, if we have to." He looked less than impressed with that idea. That was understandable, considering he might have to ask his oldest brother for a favour, and Reuben Brantley didn't do anything without a steep price tag.

"I vote we stage a breakout," Landon said. "All in favour raise your hand and say fuck yeah." The rhythm guitarist grinned and put up his hand.

"Fuck no," Penn grunted. The keyboardist was

leaning against a window frame, his ankles and arms crossed. "Then we'd all end up locked away. I spend enough time with you clowns."

"Right back at you, Penny," Asher said. "But if they lock us up, I vote for being locked up with Abbie and Zeke."

"I don't think we get to choose," Zeke said dryly, "but we're not breaking Tully out."

"Spoilsport." Landon pouted playfully.

Channing put an arm around him and patted his back. "It'll be all right. You can raise hell in some other way."

Landon's pout evaporated into a smile and he leaned over to give Channing a quick kiss.

"Don't call Zeke a spoilsport," Asher said. "That's Jackson's job."

"Thanks." Apparently Jackson got off the phone just in time to hear that remark. "The lawyer is with Tully now. All we can do is wait. And not stage a breakout." Evidently he heard that too.

"See," Asher said lightly. "Spoilsport."

I twisted around to glance at him. He looked as concerned as the rest of us. Asher used humour as a way to cope with stress. It usually helped, but today… Today everything was more difficult. More serious somehow. Ironic considering we'd spent weeks dealing with a stalker and killer who left severed heads in boxes for us to find.

Priorities.

"Did they elaborate on why they wanted to talk to Tully?" Zeke asked. "There shouldn't be a shred of evidence he had anything to do with it."

Tully was a trained assassin. He knew how to cover all of his tracks. So did the evil twins, assuming they cleaned up like they claimed they did. The fact we only had their word for that added to my unease.

"He had drinks with Xavier Lang before he died." Jackson pulled out a chair from behind the table at the side of the room and flopped down onto it. "If nothing else, Tull was one of the last people who saw him alive."

"He also gave Tully an extravagant gift," Zeke pointed out. "Killing someone isn't a standard reaction to that person giving you a record label."

"I think that's a rare enough occurrence that there is no standard reaction, as such." Penn uncrossed his ankles and crossed them the other way.

"True," Zeke conceded. "Any kind of extravagant gift. Unless they're trying to buy you off. From what Tully said, that's not the case here."

"Tully should give them Hunter and Parker's names," Penn said. "Even if they didn't kill Xavier Lang, those fuckers have plenty of blood and other shit on their hands."

No one could blame him for being bitter after the pair injected him with PCP. They left him beside a bridge he almost jumped off while high. If he ever saw them again, they'd be lucky to get out of that meeting alive. Or at least without getting punched in the face.

Hell, I'd be happy to give them a punch or two myself.

"Or Dante Fiorelli," Zeke said.

"Can we just tick an 'all of the above' box?" I asked.

"That could work," Asher agreed.

We all jumped at the sound of a knock on the door.

"I'll see who it is." Jackson sighed wearily and stood.

At this point, it could be anyone from the press, to more police, to mobsters or hitmen.

No one could say this world tour was boring.

Jackson looked through the peephole, then unlocked and opened the door.

"Levi, you're just in time for all the fun," Jackson said ironically.

Levi Jones, the owner of White Wolf Records, stepped into the room, a tired smile on his face. He was dressed in ripped black jeans, a purple T-shirt so faded I couldn't make out the logo on the front, and thick black boots. His hair was tied back in a man bun that was messier than usual. In spite of all that, he smiled and gave Jackson a bro hug.

"See, they're sleeping together," Asher whispered loudly.

I smacked him lightly in the chest with the back of my hand.

"Ouch," he said, although it couldn't possibly have hurt, since his body was rock hard. If anything, I was more likely to hurt myself by hitting him.

"I hear you guys have been raising hell," Levi said, his eyebrows raised. His gaze settled on Penn in particular.

"Not us." Penn shrugged. "We're innocent bystanders." His eyes flicked right and left as though daring us all to contradict him.

"We might not be innocent, but we're not guilty either," Zeke said. "The forces of the universe are working together to piss us off."

"It's working," Channing said dryly.

"It really is," Landon agreed. "Can't we just live our lives?"

"That doesn't seem like too much to ask," Asher said.

"It doesn't does it," I said softly.

Asher kissed my cheek. "Whatever happens, we'll deal with it like we always do. With music, alcohol and sex."

"All the good things in life." The side of Zeke's mouth tugged up adorably.

"Anyway," Levi said, having patiently waited for the banter to die down. "The lawyer thinks he can have Tully out in a couple of hours. It would be sooner, but apparently they have *paperwork*," he used finger quotes, "to do. Like any government department, the Dublin police are underfunded and under-staffed. Apparently, I could potentially face charges if I suggested a *donation* to move things along a little quicker."

"Levi Jones," Asher said, pretending to be shocked. "Did you try to bribe police officers?"

"Asher DiMarco, don't tell me you didn't think of it first," Levi retorted.

Asher chuckled and shrugged. "Of course, but Jackson didn't seem to like the idea."

"Legal channels first," Jackson said, his tone

bland. He gave Levi the side eye, apparently not approving of the mention of bribery. The band's manager had dealt with a shit ton of things since the tour started. Probably before that too, knowing the guys the way I did now. If we didn't end up locked up before the tour was over, it would probably be because of him.

"Yes." Levi moved to sit in the chair Jackson had vacated. "Legal is a lot cheaper."

"Exactly." Jackson pulled out another chair and flopped down. "You wouldn't want to end up a mere millionaire."

Levi groaned. "Definitely not. That would be terrible." He rubbed a hand across his face and smiled briefly before his expression sank back into weary frustration. "What really happened with Tully?"

"Self defence," Zeke said firmly. "Lang and a rival family, the Fiorellis, came after us. After me and my twin brothers specifically. Evidently, Xavier Lang didn't mind if Tully ended up collateral damage."

Levi winced. "Lovely. So Tully had no choice?"

"None," Zeke said. "It was him or Xavier." He still looked pissed off that anyone would do that to one of us. One of the members of his band; his real family, as far as he was concerned. As our unofficial leader, I suspected he blamed himself, even though he shouldn't. Truthfully, if it wasn't for him getting us out of the hotel in Perth just in time, things could have ended differently.

Levi nodded. "Okay." It seemed that matter was closed. He turned to Penn. "Jackson tells me you had no choice either. I've seen the photos, but I want your side of the story."

Penn uncrossed his legs and leaned his head back against the wall. "I went for a run, met up with a pair of twin assholes who thought it would be cool to inject shit into my veins. If it wasn't for Zeke, Asher and Abbie, I would have jumped into some dirty water in Mumbai, and I wouldn't be here to grace you with my presence." He smiled sardonically.

"Don't do drugs, boys and girls," Asher said.

"Nope definitely don't," Penn agreed. "Zero stars, cannot recommend. Also, stay away from evil twins."

"Naughty twins are a lot better," Levi said. He gave a slight wiggle of his eyebrows, but he was obviously troubled by everything he heard. That was understandable, it was all very troubling. Not to mention how much money he would lose if the rest of the tour was cancelled.

I mean, that wasn't the most important thing

here, but no doubt he would take it into consideration.

"Do we get to hear that story one day?" Landon asked. "About the naughty twins."

Levi laughed. "Not a chance. You'll have to use your imagination."

"My imagination is pretty good," Landon said. "Were they identical?"

"Were they male or female?" Channing asked.

Levi turned to Jackson. "I'm starting to think you're not giving them enough to do. Apparently they have nothing better to worry about than my sex life."

"I noticed that." Jackson nodded. "We could hire a personal trainer or two to make sure they get more exercise."

"They could probably practice more too," Levi said. "Wouldn't want them getting rusty, would we?"

"We definitely wouldn't." Jackson rubbed his chin as though in deep thought.

"Fine." Landon and Channing sighed almost in unison, then laughed.

"We're curious, that's all," Landon said. "Blame Asher, he's the one who started talking about it."

Asher shrugged, his chest rising and falling against my back. "I'm nosy, but I'll keep myself contained. If you insist." He made it sound like a chore as boring as hanging laundry on the line.

"We insist," Levi said. He placed his palms on the table. "Okay, I'm convinced you guys didn't get yourselves into trouble on purpose. Just… Try to stay out of it from now on, please?"

"We'll do our best," Zeke assured him. "The last thing we want is trouble." He looked tired and over it. We all were.

Levi nodded sharply and stood. "Jackson and I are going to go to the police station and see if we can get Tully out a bit sooner. We'll also speak to the press. Footage of him getting into that cop car has gone viral, as you can imagine. We'll put out that spot fire and hope that's the last of them."

His eyes lingered on me. "Are you doing okay?"

"Yeah." I nestled deeper into Asher's arms. "I'll be better if things calm down, but hopefully after this they will." I would be ecstatic if we didn't have to deal with any more attacks, murders, stalkers, and could just enjoy the rest of the tour. A little bit of boring wouldn't go astray here and there.

"Good." He smiled. "Your new single, 'Inside Out', is making us all a lot of money. Radio stations and streaming services are already clamouring for a follow-up."

That was the best news I heard all day, by far. "Thank you. If you hadn't put your faith in me…" Shit, now I was getting choked up. I blinked back tears.

"You deserve it," Levi said. "Now, you guys concentrate on the tour and we will deal with the police and media." He nodded to Jackson and they both hurried out the door.

I hoped it was as easy as he made it sound.

2

ABBIE

"At least they got Tully's angles right," Landon remarked.

"He looks good," I agreed, nodding at the footage on the television of Tully leaving the police station. He gave the cameras a brief wave, but Jackson and Levi were the ones who did the talking.

"He was never a suspect," Levi said. "The Perth police were trying to establish a timeline of events. They might have gotten a little overzealous in bringing him in, but that's all there is to it. We won't be pursuing the issue further. Thank you." He herded Tully and Jackson to a waiting car and the news broadcast changed to another story.

"Do you think that's really all there is to it?" I sat

on the end of one of the beds in the hotel room we all shared.

Landon sat behind me, a leg to either side of my hips, and massaged my back and shoulders.

Channing sat beside us, the remote for the TV in his hand. He changed the channel to some kind of cartoon and tossed the remote on the bed beside him.

"We'll find out when Tully gets back," Channing said.

"It won't be long now." Landon swept the hair off the back of my neck and planted a kiss there.

In one of the universe's giant coincidences, a knock on the door sounded about nine seconds later.

"I'll check who it is." Zeke got up from where he and Asher were cuddling on another one of the beds. He walked over to the door, each step careful, body angled back like it might explode in his face.

Hell, considering some of the shit that happened over the last few weeks, it might.

He put his eye to the peephole, then unlocked and opened the door.

By some miracle, none of us died, or were even attacked. There wasn't even a cardboard box lying in wait outside. Not one I could see anyway.

Instead, Tully strode in like nothing happened. "Hey."

"Tully!" Asher jumped up and gave him a big, warm squishy hug.

Tully hugged him back, slightly less squishy. "Anyone would think I was gone for a year."

"You could have been gone for life," Penn said dryly.

"Not a chance," Tully scoffed.

Zeke looked out into the corridor before closing the door and locking it again. "It's good to see you, bro." He also gave Tully a hug. "What did the cops want?"

Tully walked over to sit on the other side of me. "They wanted to know if I knew anything about what happened to Da... Xavier Lang. Apparently the police in Perth were aware he was into some shady shit. They thought I might know something about it. Of course, I knew nothing about it. I'm just a grieving son." He rolled his eyes and smirked.

I put a hand on his thigh. "You are, in a way. You cared about him." I searched his face for the truth of that. I found it in his eyes, but something else too. The beginning edge of acceptance. He'd started to put the night behind him, not let it haunt him any longer. Maybe the police did him a favour, pushing him to confront what happened in a way we hadn't.

He put his hand over mine. "I did, until he tried to kill me. You could say I'm grieving the man I thought he was, but if I'm honest with myself, I wasn't that blind. I mean, adopting a kid and then training him to be an assassin is a pretty big red flag." His wide mouth turned down.

"Just a bit," I agreed. I wanted to tell him that Xavier must have cared about him, at least on some level, but he was right. Trying to kill him was always going to put a dampener on that relationship. Attempted murder was something most people didn't recover from.

I held a grudge against people who did less to me. Although, they were all dead now, so I guess I could let that grudge go. Hopefully he could do the same.

"So the cops don't want anything else?" Zeke asked.

Tully turned to him. "No. They were even nice enough to apologise for the inconvenience they caused us all. They didn't go as far as to admit it, but they could have just taken me aside for a minute to ask me what they had to ask me. I think they felt bad about all the hassle."

"How big of them," Penn said sarcastically. He

was lying on another of the beds, his hands under his head, knees bent and crossed. He could have been lying on a beach, not a hotel room in Dublin. "Are you going to sue their asses?"

"Honestly, I couldn't be bothered," Tully said wearily. "It would be a pain in ass, and I don't need the money. Besides, something good did come out of it."

"Yeah, you got a hug from me when you walked through the door," Asher joked.

"Two good things then," Tully said. He smiled at me. "If the press are talking about me, then they're leaving Abbie alone."

That was true, I supposed, if beside the point.

"I can think of better silver linings," I said. "Like they could talk about someone that wasn't anyone in this room, or known to anyone in this room. Or better yet, start talking about important things like climate change, or the price of bacon."

"Huh. I didn't realise you had a problem with the price of bacon." Landon cocked his head at me and frowned.

I laughed softly. "I don't, I just think it's more important than I am. I mean, it is bacon."

"I never thought I'd say this," Asher said, a frown

on his face, "but there are more important things in life than bacon."

Grinning, Zeke pressed the back of his hand to Asher's forehead. "Are you feeling okay?"

Asher grabbed Zeke's wrist and pulled his hand down to kiss his palm. "I'm feeling fine. I just think Abbie is more important than bacon, that's all. Do you disagree?"

"Hell no." Zeke snaked an arm around Asher's neck and pulled him in for a kiss. "I think you're both more important than bacon."

"That's a stretch," Penn said. "Abbie's more important than bacon, but I don't know about you two." He smiled at the pair, who flipped him off.

"Zeke tastes better than bacon," Asher said.

Penn grimaced. "TMI. Waaay too much information."

"Asher tastes better than bacon too," Zeke said loudly.

"You're both right," I said.

Penn looked over at me. "But I taste the best, right?"

"Or me," Tully said.

I opened my mouth, but a knock on the door saved me from having to answer.

Zeke sighed. "I'll see who it is." He got back up

and trudged to the door. A moment later, he opened it to Jackson and Levi.

Levi rubbed his hands together. "What are you all doing moping around? We're in Dublin! Let's go out, have a nice dinner and enjoy ourselves."

We all stared at him.

"We're allowed out?" Asher looked amazed, if a bit sceptical.

"I don't see why not," Levi said. "We might get a bit of interest from paparazzo if they're around, but it's past time they started to report on you guys being on tour. They seem to have conveniently forgotten that, amongst all the other shit that's gone on. Let's go and party like rock stars!"

Penn picked his head up and looked at Levi. "Can we get changed first?"

We were all dressed in the clothes we'd travelled to Dublin in. Some of the guys wore track pants or jeans, but a couple of us, like me, wore shorts. I preferred skirts, but it wasn't always easy to find somewhere to do laundry while on tour, so shorts it was for now. The ones I wore were bright pink with purple flowers. Definitely not a rock star look.

Well, unless you were the kind of rock star who entertained children with songs about dinosaurs and brightly coloured convertible cars. Then they were perfect.

"Sure," Levi said cheerfully. "Knock yourselves out. But don't take too long." He leaned back against the door and crossed his arms.

Jackson shrugged. "You heard the boss. It's time for some fun. And before Asher says anything, yes, I know how to have fun." He smirked at Asher.

Asher grinned. "I wasn't even thinking that."

"You would have," Jackson told him.

"Well… Yeah," Asher conceded. "I probably would."

"You definitely would." Zeke patted him on the shoulder. "That's one of the things we love about you." They both went for their suitcases and started to get changed.

I exhaled and moved down the bed a centimetre or two before Tully caught my hand in his.

"Can I talk to you for a minute?" he asked. His wide mouth was pressed in a line so tight his lips were pale.

"Of course you can," I said. I flashed Landon a smile of gratitude for his massage. The guy had magical fingers.

My hand in Tully's, I let him lead me over to the corner of the room.

"Are you okay?" I asked. It was strange to check in with him like that. It was usually the guys asking me. The expression on his face had me worried though.

What could he possibly have to tell me that would make him look like that?

"Yes, I'm fine," he said quickly. "When I got into the back of that cop car, I started to think about what would happen if things didn't work out all right. For all I knew, they had CCTV footage of me and Xavier. I knew they didn't, I looked, but you know how the mind likes to play tricks on us." He shrugged a single shoulder.

"I absolutely do know," I said wryly. "The twins could have done something again."

"That occurred to me too," he agreed. "Plus the Fiorellis and Brantleys have long arms. Dante Fiorelli in particular might be pissed I ended his new lapdog."

He sounded so bitter my heart ached for him.

He closed his brown eyes for a moment before he continued. "For a while there, I wasn't sure if I would walk away from the police station. And that got me thinking about not seeing you every day. That would have been the worst part of this. Even worse than never playing guitar again."

I wound my arms around his neck. "Thank goodness none of that happened."

He slipped his arms around me and buried his face in my neck. "I would have gone crazy. But worst of all, if anything happened to me, I wouldn't have told you I love you. I need you to know that. I'm head over heels, madly in love with you."

My heart skipped a beat. I held him tight, like I planned to never let go. "I love you too."

I hadn't thought about what would happen if I never see him again. I hadn't seriously considered the possibility. Now I did, my heart ached even harder. I resolved to do whatever I could to make sure that never actually happened.

"I don't know what I would have done if I hadn't met you guys," I said softly. "You've all become so important to me."

That was an understatement. I couldn't imagine not seeing them every day and being in their lives. And in their beds. In the short time I'd known them, they'd become everything to me. My world. There was nothing I wouldn't do to be with them, including giving up music.

A few weeks ago, nothing would have made me even consider thinking about that. Now, it seemed so insignificant, in the scheme of things. I loved music, but it wasn't my universe anymore.

"We would have tracked you down," Tully said with absolute certainty. "Something would have brought us together. It was as inevitable as breathing. As the sun rising in the morning."

"As you walking out of that police station," I said.

"More inevitable than that," he said. "It was the most inevitable of inevitabilities."

"That's almost as much a mouthful as you are," I said.

His chest rumbled against mine. "Almost. That's a pretty high bar."

I snorted. What was it with guys and their cocks? It was almost like they were really fond of them or something.

Okay, why shouldn't they be? I certainly was.

"Yes it is," I said. And it was.

All of the guys were impressive. I knew that from first-hand experience with four of them. I was sure I'd find the same with Landon and Channing when we got around to it. None of these guys could disappoint me if they tried. The best part about that—I knew they wouldn't try. They wanted to make me as happy as I wanted to make them.

"We should go and make ourselves pretty," I said finally.

"Too late," Tully said. "You're already pretty."

"No, you," I said back.

"No, you." He grinned.

We went on like that while we got ready to go out and enjoy the city.

3

LANDON

"I FEEL like we've been let out of confinement." I sipped my beer and grinned at Channing and Abbie. What could be better than sitting in a genuine Irish pub in Ireland with my favourite people in the whole wide world?

Like always, I sat next to Channing, but we managed to snag a spot next to Abbie.

He and I were both as into her as the rest of the guys, but we agreed to sit back and take it slowly. Partly because we both wanted to get to know her and partly because we'd been so tight for the last two years, we didn't want to screw up our dynamic with each other.

Lately though, the three of us had become closer. The progression from friends to potentially something more felt natural and comfortable. Which was just how I liked things. Was a relationship real if you had to force it? Nah.

"I'm surprised Zeke let us out," Channing said. He gave our lead singer the side eye.

"Is Zeke the boss?" Levi asked. He looked and sounded buzzed already.

We looked at Zeke, then at Levi. In unison, we said, "Yes!"

Everyone at the table laughed except Levi, who was pretending to look put out.

"Wrong answer."

Zeke shrugged and sipped his bourbon and cola like, well, like a boss. "I've trained them well."

Asher slung an arm over his shoulders. "Yes, you have. So well that when Levi tells us to go out and have a good time, we do. But we make sure it's okay with you first."

They shared a brief kiss.

They were almost as cute together as Channing and I. Yeah, that was a very high bar. We were pretty fucking adorable. We also knew there was something between Asher and Zeke long before they did. It took meeting Abbie to bring them together, but they would have gotten there sooner or later.

Even if we had to give them a kick in the ass to get going.

"Do they do what you say?" Levi asked Jackson.

Jackson snorted. "Only if they were planning to do it in the first place. I didn't have any grey hairs until I started managing them."

"That's bullshit," Penn said. He was drinking cola without any alcohol.

I suspected his run in with the evil twins had him twitchy about any kind of drugs. As long as I'd known him, he'd never been a big drinker anyway, but now he seemed particularly cautious. Maybe he was on his guard against Hunter and Parker, who would undoubtedly turn up sooner or later. I wouldn't want to be them when they did. We all wanted to punch the shit out of them.

"You had grey hairs when we met you," Penn added.

The guy had absolutely no filter whatsoever. It was refreshing sometimes and irritating at others. I loved him like a brother, just like I loved the rest of the band.

I wanted to punch him out sometimes too.

"Thanks Penn, I appreciate it," Jackson said sarcastically. "You're as sweet as always."

"You're welcome." Penn gave him a sardonic

smile. "I'm always ready to dish out a healthy dose of reality for anyone who needs it." He looked around the table. "Anyone else?"

"I think we've all had enough reality lately," Tully said. He looked tired. He hadn't been himself since that night in Perth.

I guessed killing the guy who raised you for most of your life would do that to a person. I wished I knew what to say or do to make it better. Apart from being a trained assassin, Tully was one of the gentlest people I knew. I also knew Abbie was helping him out a lot, being there for him and giving him cuddles. Sometimes, that was all you could do.

"More than enough reality," Abbie agreed.

She looked tired too, but as beautiful as ever. I never saw eyes that shade of blue before. They were an even better shade than my hair. I mean, my hair looked pretty awesome, but there was no comparison. Just looking at her made my cock hard. Looking at Channing did the same thing.

Although, I was twenty-two. Pretty much everything made my cock hard.

I leaned over in my chair and brushed my lips over hers. She tasted like citrus from the vodka and lemon she was drinking, only sweeter.

"From now on, let's make a pact to have as much

fun as we can." I leaned the other way and kissed Channing. He tasted like beer, which was just as delicious.

"Hell yeah, I'm in," Channing said without hesitation.

I wouldn't have expected anything else from him. Whenever one of us suggested something, the other was right by his side, ready to jump feet-first.

The rest of the guys thought we were joined at the hip. We might as well have been sometimes. Tully would have said something about the universe making us for each other and bringing us together. That sounded about right to me.

The more I got to know her, the more I thought Abbie belonged in that picture too. And all the other guys, but them in a platonic way. Not that they weren't adorable, but I wasn't into any of them and they weren't into me either, as far as I knew. That arrangement worked for everyone.

"I'm always down for having fun," Abbie said. "We haven't had enough of it recently."

I smiled. "I was hoping you'd say that. While we were waiting for Tully, I did a search on my phone. I found a place you might find interesting. If the zookeepers will let us out, that is." I glanced over at Zeke and Levi.

It was Zeke who responded. "It depends what it is. And where it is. You know the rule about not going off anywhere by yourself."

It was difficult not to chafe at that and tell him to fuck off. I knew he was trying to take care of us all and keep us safe, but we were adults. We could make our own choices.

On the other hand, we also didn't want to end up dead or arrested. That would suck. Not in a good way.

"Just down the block," I said lightly. "We could walk there from here. We could all go." My gaze shifted to Abbie. I really wanted to have her and Channing alone for a while. And away from a hotel room or a stage.

On the other hand, if the others wanted to come and watch… That kind of was the point.

"There's enough of us," Channing said. "We can take care of ourselves and each other." The whole 'being locked away from the world' thing annoyed him more than it annoyed me. He didn't like being told what to do and he didn't like sitting still for too long. He preferred to be active and busy. He was always looking for his next distraction or adventure. If one didn't find him, he got short-tempered and edgy.

I loved him for it; it was who he was, but when he went off by himself in the Mumbai airport and we thought he was dead...

I was happy to follow Zeke's rules if it meant keeping Channing in my line of sight, and out of trouble, or a grave.

The thought of losing him scared the shit out of me. Honestly, the thought of losing any of them scared the shit out of me. That was one of the many reasons why Abbie was so perfect for us. If our lives centred around her, and each other, then we would never need or want to leave each other for other people.

If that was how it worked out, I'd be a happy boy.

Zeke sighed. "Fine, we'll go, but keep your eyes open for twin motherfuckers who might have a passing resemblance to me, and don't talk to anyone who looks like paparazzi."

"When would we ever talk to anyone who looks like paparazzi?" Channing asked.

I pointed at my boyfriend. "What he said. Unless Jackson told us to." After a moment I added, "Or Levi."

"At least you got the order right," Jackson said. He smiled slyly.

Levi snorted. "I get no respect. None. Hey Tully, I

hear you scored your own record label. Let's talk later."

Tully did a double-take at the sudden change of subject. "Right. Sure." He looked like he didn't have a clue what Levi would have to say, but in typical Tully style, he had an open mind. Honestly, when it came to Levi, that was the best way to be.

"Maybe he wants to tell you all about how you won't get any respect from anyone signed with your label," Asher said jokingly.

"Tully will totally get respect from them," Penn said.

Now we were all surprised. Since when did Penn start sticking up for Tully? Or anyone else for that matter? He was usually ready with an insult, not praise or support. Knowing Abbie must have changed him too.

Tully shrugged. "A guy can hope. Maybe we should start giving Levi more respect."

"Hell yeah," Levi said. He raised his nearly-empty glass at that.

At the same time, everyone else said, "Nah," and laughed.

Abbie leaned over and stretched out so she could put a hand on Levi's arm. "You know we all love you, right?" Of course, she'd be the sweet one and reach out to him.

"We really do." Asher nodded his agreement, but a cheeky smile tugged at the corners of his mouth. "If we didn't like you, we'd be nice to you." He gave in to the urge to grin broadly. His eyes shone with humour and sass.

"We wouldn't want that, would we?" Levi said ironically. "Lucky for you, I'm a big boy. I can take it. It's not like you assholes give me a choice anyway."

He gulped his drink, swallowing down so much, I was worried he'd choke on it. Somehow, he didn't.

"Not really," Zeke agreed. "You learn to roll with it after a while." He made a face like he was one long-suffering dude, and sighed dramatically.

"When do you not get respect?" I asked Zeke.

"All the time," Zeke said offhandedly. He frowned as though deep in thought. "I can't think of any specific occasions right now." A smile caught at the corners of his mouth and his brows twitched once, twice. Not quite a wiggle, but close enough.

"You're so full of shit," Penn told him scathingly. "Everyone respects you, and you know it."

"Being called full of shit is, um, a good example of not getting respect," Zeke pointed out. He cocked his head at Penn and raised his eyebrows to their full height. His mouth jerked to one side.

"Nah," Penn said. "I'm just being honest." He sipped his cola and shrugged. He would never be apologetic for calling someone a fucking idiot, much less telling them they're full of shit.

That was Penn for you.

Zeke and Asher exchanged a look and shrugged. We had all learned long ago not to take anything Penn said personally. Just like Penn didn't take anything we said personally. Giving each other shit was part of who we were as a group.

Brothers onstage and off. For better or worse. Richer or… even richer. And so on.

Channing caught my eye as he swallowed the last of his beer. "I'm ready to get out of here," he said

The side of his mouth twitched, a subtle sign of his agitation. When we made a plan to go somewhere, he pretty much had to go right now, if not sooner. It was an impulse for him, something he couldn't get past.

I learned to roll with it a long time ago. It was just another adorable thing about him. One of many.

I nodded and downed my last mouthful, then held the glass up for the last drop. I didn't want to waste perfectly good beer, did I now? Nope, I didn't.

I leaned over to Abbie. "Are you ready?" I gave her a look to suggest I didn't just mean ready to leave the pub. I was ready to have a good time with her and get closer to her.

Okay, I wanted to fuck her and Channing. My cock twitched at the thought of it. My balls felt so heavy they might fall off if they waited much longer. That would suck six ways from Sunday.

Her cheeks turned an adorable shade of pink. "I'm ready," she said softly.

"Don't worry," I said "We've got you."

"I know you do," she said. "I trust you."

That warmed my heart and my balls at the same time. Having her trust meant so much to me.

I was painfully aware I was the youngest guy in the band. The one everyone might assume would flake out, or do something stupid. To have her believe in me…

I might have puffed my chest out a little.

"I won't let you down," I promised.

4

ABBIE

"THIS IS THE PLACE." Landon waved towards a stairway that led down into what sounded like a basement club. Throbbing music pumped out toward us.

I admit to being a little nervous. I wasn't sure what Landon had in mind, except for one thing. I was at least ninety-nine percent sure it involved sex. With Landon. And Channing.

The guys told me right from the start they were never with a woman unless they were both involved. I'd seen myself how committed they were to each other. Being with someone else without the other around must feel like cheating to them.

What did that mean when it came to me being with the other guys without everyone being there? I hadn't been with only one guy since Penn and I had our hate fuck up against the wall in the stadium in Seoul. It was usually me with Zeke and Asher or me with Tully and Penn. Tully and Penn didn't touch each other, but they enjoyed sharing me as much as I did.

"This might be the seediest fucking place I've ever seen," Asher remarked. "I like it."

"That's because you're a degenerate," Zeke teased. He draped an arm over Asher's shoulders. "Just like me."

"Which is why we're so good for each other," Asher said.

"Does that make me a degenerate too?" I asked sweetly. I knew they weren't implying anything, but I couldn't resist stirring them up. Their constant banter and razzing was rubbing off on me. Or maybe I felt comfortable enough around them to be myself for the first time in a long time.

Landon put an arm around my waist and another around Channing's and tucked each of us against his hips. "It makes you whatever you want to be," he said firmly.

We started down the stairs in lockstep with each other.

The further we went, the harder the music

throbbed. It pounded through my feet, pulsed through my stomach and the rest of my body.

I loved feeling music as much as I loved hearing it. There was something compelling about a bass so heavy you couldn't tell it apart from your own heartbeat. Maybe they were in sync. Maybe I was inside the music. Maybe it was inside me.

The bouncers on the door barely gave us more than a glance and a nod before we headed through the door. If they recognised us, they knew better than to stare.

I realised the reason for that the moment I stepped inside.

The lights were low, like you'd expect from a nightclub. It took my eyes a couple of minutes to adjust.

"Oh my," I said in a voice even I couldn't really hear.

Everywhere I looked, everything was either black or gold. A few people sat or stood with drinks in their hands, shouting to be heard over the music. Others were lying on couches, clothes half off, hands and mouths all over each other.

It reminded me of the club Tully took me to in Perth, but instead of private rooms, people were just… fucking.

"Like I said, my kind of place," Asher shouted over the music.

"Mine too," Penn shouted. He liked to watch, but not as much as he liked to take part.

Landon drew me to him so he could speak in my ear and be heard. "How do you feel about doing it in front of other people? It's kinda a thing for me. Don't worry about anyone here taking photos and telling the press. The owners of places like this keep a super close eye on everything. Besides, people would have to admit they were here too." He grinned.

"That's a good point," I said. I nodded and tried to tear my eyes away from the woman who was bent over a table, a slender man thrusting into her like he planned to take all night and then some.

People came to clubs like this to explore a side of themselves they wouldn't explore out in the real world. They certainly wouldn't admit to it. That explained why the bouncers didn't look too closely. Discretion was currency in clubs like this. See nothing, know nothing, tell the paparazzi nothing.

Fucking perfect. Mental chef's kiss to the establishment. More places should be like this.

"So… What do you think? No pressure to do anything you don't want to do." Landon squeezed my hand and gave me a reassuring smile.

Honestly, between the music, the people clearly enjoying themselves, and being surrounded by six hot guys, I was dripping wet already. All I wanted, right this moment, was to be touched and to touch.

The idea of doing that in front of strangers added an extra thrill. I liked screwing in front of the other guys. And there was that one time outside Zeke's place just after we met, when two guys walked past. They stopped to watch and clap.

Yeah, that was a fucking good memory. And a good fucking memory.

In the back of my mind, there was even the excited thought—what would happen if someone took a photo of us and it leaked out? No, I didn't want that to happen, but at the same time...the forbidden was arousing as hell.

"I'm game," I said finally.

Landon grinned. He took Channing and I by the hand and led us over to a corner. Zeke and Asher sat side by side on a couch nearby.

Tully and Penn went to the bar to get drinks, but made it clear they were also going to watch. Avidly, by the look of the tenting in the front of both their jeans.

They were pushed to the back of my mind as Landon sat me down between him and Channing.

I decided to let them guide me in this. Not the fucking part, I knew how to do that already. I'd even seen them do it with each other.

No, what I didn't want to do was overstep and get in the way of the relationship between the two of them. The thing between them and me was new and I was still finding my way with the boundaries. There might be things they would do with and for each other, that they wouldn't do with me.

I'd let them show me.

Landon put a hand on my cheek and kissed me lightly, then turned my face so Channing could kiss me too. Both of them had soft lips with a tickle of stubble and the taste of beer.

In spite of that, I could have closed my eyes and told you who was who from the way they felt. Channing's kisses were a little firmer, not quite possessive, but hard compared to Landon's. Landon's kisses were soft, but his tongue was more bold. It bobbed against my lower lip every time we kissed.

Both guys rested a hand on either side of my waist. In almost the exact same place. I got the impression they made sure whatever one did, the other did in equal proportion. It was sweet how considerate they were of each other, and of me.

When Landon slipped a hand up the back of my

shirt, Channing slid one up the front. Landon unhooked my bra and Channing pulled down the cups to let my breasts fall free.

I guessed they'd done that move before. Like with the other guys, I wasn't judging their pasts. Instead, I admired how well they worked together. If they practised a lot to get there, I got to reap the benefit of it.

Win.

They gripped the hem of my shirt, front and back and lifted it up to expose my breasts. My nipples immediately pebbled with the brush of cooler air, and the need to be spoilt.

I swallowed hard, and glanced up. The only ones looking at me were the guys, their gazes eager and hungry. No paparazzi popped up to take photos.

Yet.

Landon slipped a hand around the front of me to cup my breast and palm one nipple until it was harder still. Channing lapped at the other with the tip of his tongue.

I shivered deliciously, so aroused already all I knew was that and the thud of the music. Fortunately, the couch under me was the kind you could wipe down. Otherwise I would have left a permanent mark in the shape of a puddle.

I hesitated for a moment, then grabbed the hem of my shirt from where it sat just below my neck. In a quick movement, before I changed my mind, I pulled it off the rest of the way. Then my bra with it.

I set them aside on the floor beside the couch and slipped my hands up the front of Channing's T-shirt.

Like the other guys, he was ripped. Rock hard ridges were smooth under my fingers except where I encountered several scars. What were they from? I'd have to ask him some time.

I slid my hands up higher, taking his shirt with me. I'd seen him naked before, but not up this close, not touching. Now I was, I saw and felt the criss-cross of scars across his torso, interspersed with tattoos and muscle.

With one hand, he gripped his own hem and pulled his shirt off over his head in a single move-ment. His nipple ring caught the low light in the club and glittered.

Sensing it was the right thing to do, I turned to run my hands over Landon's stomach and chest and help him out of his shirt.

He gave me a smile that let me know he knew I figured out how they liked things.

I smiled back and kissed his mouth, then Channing's.

They manoeuvred me so I was reclining against the back of the couch, my feet still on the floor, and both had one of my nipples in their mouth. They were almost close enough for the tops of their heads to brush against each other if they weren't careful.

I quivered under their touch. I half closed my eyes and looked over to see Zeke and Asher making out. Penn and Tully were watching me like I was the main event on a small, intimate stage. All they needed was a bucket of popcorn between them.

It shouldn't really come as a surprise that people who performed for a living weren't shy about what they did in front of other people. If we were, we wouldn't be very good performers. The ability to sing or play music was only one part of the job. Some would argue it's not even the most important part.

I wasn't going to get involved in that argument. As far as I was concerned, it was all important.

In sync as ever, Landon and Channing both slipped a hand up my thigh. Their fingers bumped at the apex of my thighs and they both rumbled with laughter. Channing's hand retreated to the inside of my leg, while Landon brushed feather light strokes over the base of my belly and the top of my folds.

I let my hands wander and dance over the front

of each of their pants, finding twin bulges there. I wanted to feel both of them inside me.

They raised their heads and, with the stubble of their cheeks tickling my nipples, they kissed each other.

Holy shit that was hot.

Hotter still when they stretched over me and undid each other's jeans.

I looked down, watching as both erections sprang free, both dark with blood and desire. I wasn't sure if I should touch them, or if they wanted to touch each other. I got my answer when they went back to lavishing attention on my nipples and ghosting fingers over the gusset of my panties, and venturing underneath.

I curled a hand around each of their cocks and oh so slowly slid my hands down to their sacs and back up again. Landon's cock was slightly longer, and bent to the left, while Channing's was a little thicker. A Prince Albert piercing cut across the sax player's tip.

They were both hot as fuck and throbbing as though filled with the music too.

The guys exchanged a glance and a nod before putting their hands under me to lift my hips and pull down my panties.

Again, I swallowed and looked around. No one was looking at me, but two guys, women on their knees in front of them, sucking each of their cocks, looked close to coming. Their eyes were closed as they thrust their hips slowly, or we might have locked gazes.

"You're so beautiful." Landon sat up beside me and kissed my mouth. At the same time, Channing moved down to kneel between my legs.

Anticipating their next move, I slid down the back of the couch until I was lying with my head in Landon's lap, my shoulder beside his thigh.

He stroked my hair, before curling his fingers around a fistful and slipping his cock between my lips.

I tasted his pre-cum with my tongue, which I rolled over his tip and around the end of his shaft. I cupped his heavy balls lightly in my hand and massaged them before lowering my mouth fully, deeply onto his heated length.

I felt a groan pass through him, down his body, to the cheek I had pressed to the light hair of his rock hard belly.

I guessed he liked that as much as I did.

Channing started to flick against my clit with his tongue. It didn't surprise me at all that a saxophonist was good with his mouth. Better than good. He had me panting around Landon's erection in a matter of several teasing strokes

He teased me right to the edge of coming. Every nerve in my body was ready, racing toward that delicious peak. I bucked against his mouth and tightened my grip on Landon's balls. I sucked harder with every roll of my hips.

Right before the orgasm crashed over me, Channing pulled away from my clit. He kissed the insides of my thigh, down toward my knees, then back up my other leg.

I growled in frustration, slowed my sucking and caught my breath.

He smiled at me and wiggled his eyebrows. Yeah, he knew exactly what he was doing.

Clit tease.

He finally found his way back to my pussy, right before I suggested he get a map, but instead of spoiling my poor clit, he tickled my rear hole with his tongue, and lapped all around my folds.

Everywhere but my clit.

Should I order him around like Penn did to me? I would in a minute, if he didn't stop driving me crazy.

He glanced up at me, a knowing smile in his eyes,

before he finally went back to lapping at my clit and sliding his tongue inside me.

I wasn't starting from scratch, but he'd neglected my clit for long enough that it took several minutes to work back to where I was. I decided it was worth it. The second time felt even better than the first. My nerves were singing in time to the music, more intense, more *ready* than before.

I ground against his tongue, moaning when he slid a couple of skilled fingers inside me to stroke my g-spot.

Fuck, yes. I would have shouted if my mouth wasn't full, but I did moan and graze my teeth over Landon's cock.

His hand tightened around my hair. He must be close too.

The orgasm slipped up like a tiger creeping through a darkened jungle, padding it way on huge, soft paws to find me. Just before it pounced, Channing drew back again.

"Fucking hell," I said around Landon's cock.

Laughter rumbled through Landon's belly and into my face. He was lucky I only bit down on him gently.

Landon bent down toward my ear. "That feels amazing, honey."

Well, if he liked that… I bit down a little harder, nibbling gently on his hot skin.

"Ah yeah," he groaned.

I glanced down to Channing, who didn't even look slightly sorry for frustrating the crap out of me. Instead, he was busy running his tongue over the tender flesh on the inside of my thigh and pretending he was innocent of any wrongdoing.

He even lifted his mouth just high enough for me to see his cheeky grin.

When he lowered his face again, it was to thoroughly kiss the insides of both my thighs.

I was so frustrated by now, I was ready to scream.

I dropped my hand toward my clit, intending to get myself off, but Channing caught my wrist and held it a couple of centimetres away.

He shook his head and gave me a scolding look, before finally returning his attention where it belonged, my poor hungry, begging clit.

This time it wasn't a tiger, it was a whole streak of them. They leapt on me so hard, I couldn't have fought them off if I tried. Every single nerve in my body exploded with a rush of pleasure that thundered louder than the pounding music around me.

Nothing—*nothing* existed in the entire world but

the pulsing, throbbing heat of blood, orgasm, strobing lights and the shatter of my being into infinity, amazing fucking pieces. I shuddered and screamed and bit, maybe too hard.

I was barely down before the tigers pounced again, even more unrelentless than before. I sobbed and gasped, overwhelmed by sensation. The blood in my ears drowned out the thudding music. I arched my back and had to slide my mouth off Landon's cock so I could catch half a ragged breath before crashing back down to Earth in a puddle of boneless skin.

Channing went on licking and teasing until I came all the way down and wriggled with the sensitivity of my clit.

He lifted his face, shining with my juices, and smiled like the cat that licked up *all* of the cream. Which was basically accurate.

Like a tag team, Landon slipped away from me and they swapped places.

Landon knelt between my knees and positioned his cock at my entrance.

Channing replaced Landon's cock in my mouth with his.

Like their lips, their cocks tasted different. Landon's was sweeter, but Channing's had a unique flavour that made my tongue sing. Although, I was tempted to bite him hard for edging me. Okay, it was worth it, so he got a pass.

This time.

Landon slowly slid his cock inside my body, all the way to the hilt.

I sighed with pleasure, tingled with the aftermath of coming, and the other people fucking around us. Add the pumping music and every nerve in my body was flooded. It could have overwhelmed me, but it was like a perfect symphony of sensation. It was..... freeing in a way I never felt before.

Like everything so far, when they fucked my mouth and pussy, they did it in near-perfect sync. At the same time, they angled their upper bodies so they could kiss, tangling tongues over my head. Landon had one hand on my hip and the other on Channing's arm. Channing had a hand on Landon's back and the other on the back of my neck. It was like being tied in a perfect knot.

I managed a quick glance over to see Zeke and Asher lying top to tail on their couch, cocks in each other's mouths.

Penn and Tully both had theirs in their hands, eyes still on me. Penn locked his eyes on me and came as I watched. My eyes widened and I almost did the same. It wasn't until a few moments later when Tully came that a light orgasm fluttered through me, making me tingle and convulse around Landon's cock.

He must have been close to the edge already, because he came right behind me, gasping and thrusting furiously, teeth gritted in concentration, lips apart. He let out a choked cry and dug his fingers into my hips. He scrunched up his face and thrust more slowly, before finally coming to a stop.

I sucked Channing harder, encouraging him to come too. He grunted and rolled his hips, thrusting faster, then slower, then faster again, like he was needing to come but wanting to delay it for as long as he could.

I was tempted to pull my mouth off him and let him be frustrated for a while, but instead I grazed my teeth along his length and pumped him with my hand and mouth.

"Oh, fuck," he shouted. "Fuck, fuck, fuck." He grabbed the back of my head in both hands and pulled me down harder onto his cock, until he was right at the back of my throat.

I sucked until my mouth hurt, then went and sucked until he exploded inside me, flooding my throat with his pearly juices.

He held me there while he milked himself for every last drop, then finally let me go.

I pulled off him, swallowed hard, and gasped for air.

"Wow." Landon nestled up against me on the couch, fully naked. "I knew you would fit with us."

"Yeah," Channing agreed. "Perfect fit." He flopped down on the other side of me, not beside Landon for once.

At that moment, their two became three. Another piece of our puzzle.

5

ABBIE

"HAVE YOU EVER PLAYED BASS GUITAR?" Landon looked at me from under his ridiculously long eyelashes.

The only way I could have lashes like that would be with extensions. Mine were so short and light, they all but disappeared against my face unless I wore mascara.

"Never," I replied. "I've played guitar, but never bass. Is it hard?" I should know better than to ask a question like that. I really should.

The minute I did, he grinned. "Usually. Especially around you and Channing."

Channing, who was on the other side of the stage, changing the reed in his saxophone, must have heard his name. He looked up briefly and smiled before he looked back down again. The only time they weren't side-by-side, apart from the other night, was when they were on stage. Then they were all about the music.

I rolled my eyes playfully. "Sorry, I should have asked if it's difficult compared to playing a regular guitar?" Sometimes I felt like I was surrounded by a pack of horny boys. Then I remembered I liked that about them.

Landon picked up his bright purple bass and plucked a couple of strings. They left out a soft twang.

"It's not that much different, to be honest. It has fewer strings and a lower pitch, as you know." He glanced slyly at Tully. "And my instrument is bigger."

Tully arched an eyebrow at him and paused in tuning his own, black, electric guitar. "Only your guitar," he said dryly.

"Keep telling yourself that," Landon teased. He held his bass out to me. "You wanna try?"

I eyed him and his instrument—the musical one —with scepticism. "It's not that I don't want to, it's just that there's already hundreds of fans lined up outside the front of the venue. I wouldn't want to scare them away with my shitty playing."

It was a beautiful morning in Paris, if a little

chilly. Europe was a refreshing change after Asia, at least in climate.

"They might shout 'merde' and run away." That was one of the few words I knew in French, apart from baguette, fromage and croissant. And oui, of course. All of the most important ones.

Landon laughed. "It's not plugged in. No one will hear it but us. I'll plug it in before the sound check starts."

The staff who worked on the tour were still busy running around, setting up the stage. The sound guys in particular were fiddling around with the speakers to take best advantage of the acoustics.

I liked to watch them work, their level of dedication was incredible, and of course they made us sound good. Some days, that was miraculous.

"Okay." I took the bass from him. "I better not break this then."

He gave me a face that suggested no, I fucking better not. Guys and their instruments were like guys and their cocks. Any damage to either would cause a lot of pain. Some of them looked after their instruments better than themselves. Fair enough, when your livelihood depended on it.

The bass was heavier than I expected, but still comfortable in my arms. When I was a kid, I used to accompany myself on an old acoustic guitar my parents bought me from a garage sale. It quickly became obvious I was better at singing than I was at playing, at least at a professional level, but I enjoyed it regardless. I mean, you don't have to be good at a thing to get pleasure from it. Right?

I strummed a few chords and managed not to make the guitar sound like a dying duck. Honestly, considering what it was worth, it wouldn't sound bad unless the player really sucked, but it would sound better in the hands of someone like Landon. Someone with talent, skill and dedication. Not to mention magical hands.

"When did you start playing?" I asked curiously.

"I don't remember not playing," he said, a faint frown on his brow. "Mum and I had instruments lying around from her boyfriends. A couple of them left them behind when they ditched on her." The side of his mouth pulled back and his eyes glazed.

"Assholes never stuck around for very long." They were clearly unpleasant memories. His anger at the past wasn't buried deep. Right now, he wore every moment of it on his face.

I paused in my strumming. I wanted to kiss away his pain, but the darkness wasn't so easily vanquished. "I'm so sorry. That must have been difficult." My heart broke a little for the kid who must have wondered why people came and went from his life so quickly.

He shrugged. "I can't say I blame them. She was into a bunch of shit. Crack, usually. She used to leave me alone at night so she could go out and... Do what she had to do to get money for it. And to buy food once in a while. Took me the longest fucking time to realise she was selling herself." He swiped the back off his hand over his cheek, but not before I saw a tear glisten there.

My mouth formed an O. "That's terrible. How old were you?"

"I dunno." He flopped down on Penn's bench. "About eight or nine. One of the neighbours found out and dobbed on her. Cops came and I went into foster care. Lucky they let me take a guitar with me. I probably would have gone ballistic without it."

"Yeah, I'm sure you would." I placed his bass down as carefully as if it was mine, and sat beside him, my thigh touching his.

"I've always found music the best way to escape reality." I wound an arm around him and leaned against his shoulder.

"Exactly." He nodded his agreement. "Anyway, Mum tried to get clean and get me back. It worked for a while, but eventually she went back to her old ways." He sighed heavily. "I went back into foster care until I met this mob." He gestured briefly around the stage with his hand. "They kinda saved me, y'know?"

"I do know," I agreed. "They've saved me too. A few times. Them and you. It seems to be something you guys do. You might be superheroes in disguise." I gave him a teasing, speculative look, laced with sympathy for kid-Landon and even past me, who needed saving so badly.

He managed a faint smile. "That sounds about right. They're a good bunch to fall in with."

I smiled softly and kissed his cheek. "They really are. Even Penn."

Penn, who was lying on the front of the stage, his hands under his head, looked over at us. "Especially Penn," he said before he closed his eyes again. "Also, you're on my bench."

"You'll live, mate," Landon said, shrugging indifferently.

"Can I ask what happened to your mother?" I said gently. "Is she still…"

"Alive? Using?" He shrugged. "I couldn't tell ya. I tried to keep in touch with her, but she drops in and out. Last time I heard from her was about six months ago. She told me she was trying to get clean. I wanted to believe her but I've heard it a thousand times before. At this point, it is what it is. I've tried to help her, but she has to help herself first."

"She has to *want* to," Penn said. "No one could make me do shit until I was ready." He turned his face towards us. He would have denied it, but he had sympathy in his eyes. If anyone would have a clue what Landon went through, he would.

"The struggle is real," Landon said. "I just had to learn to get on with it and not think about it too much. Not dwell on it and shit."

I reached around with both arms and gave him a squeeze. "It sucks that you have to do that. People talk about how important family is, but so often family isn't people you are related to by blood. Is it?"

"Nope," he agreed. "My sperm donor wasn't much fuckin' help either. He skipped out before I was born. Fuck only knows what his name was, Mum would never tell me. Truth is, she probably didn't know." He exhaled as though he wanted to blow his frustrations out his mouth and away. "Honestly, I'm not gonna lose any sleep over it. Not anymore."

"You used to?" I asked softly.

"Totally," he agreed. He hesitated for a moment as though unsure how I'd react to what he was about to say. Finally, he continued, "I still lie awake at night and wish he'd come and take me away to some, I don't know, superyacht or fancy island, or superhero lair. Or, like, anything really. That probably sounds dumb as shit."

"It sounds totally normal to me," I said. "I used to wish the same thing. Not for a father to take me away. Mine was all right."

I smiled ruefully, embarrassed at kid-me. "I used to wish for some rich, hot guy who would carry me away and worship me." That wasn't too much to ask, right? After a moment I added, "Now I have six."

Hell yeah. Maybe kid-me wasn't so crazy after all.

"Fuck," Landon said, a frown on his adorable face.

I sat up. "What? Is something wrong?"

"Yeah," he said slowly. "I forgot to buy a superyacht. What a letdown." He smiled.

I laughed and smacked him lightly on the chest. "I don't need a superyacht. Or a fancy island. Or even a superhero lair. Although, that would be cool." I mean, who wouldn't want one of those?

"Oh, man. Now I want to get a superyacht to sail off to a fancy island that has a superhero lair on it." He grinned.

"You're gonna get kicked out of the band if you keep being nerdy like that," Penn remarked.

"You might get kicked out of the band if you're not nerdy enough," Asher said as he and Zeke stepped out onto the stage.

"Yeah," Zeke agreed. "There's nothing wrong with being nerdy. Or geeky."

"The fuck kind of rock gods are you guys?" Penn asked. He rolled his eyes, but smiled slightly.

"The nerdy kind, obviously," Asher said. He stepped over and gave me a kiss before moving to sit behind his drums.

"The kind who are ready for a sound check," Zeke said. He waved for everyone to get up and get into place.

Landon stood, but before I could, Penn waved me back down. "You can stay if you want to."

He'd come a long way from a couple of months ago, when he told me to get the fuck off the stage during Wolf Venom's sound check. Back then, he seemed to hate the sight of me. And I wanted to wipe the smirk off his face almost as much as I wanted to fuck him.

We'd both come a long way, now I thought about it.

"Okay." I sat around on the stool and played a few notes.

"Not worried about making me look bad?" He

slipped in beside me and dropped a lingering kiss on my lips.

"No," I said lightly. My mouth twitched as I struggled to hold back a smile.

He raised his eyebrows. He didn't look like he believed me.

"Are you waiting for me to say you can do that all by yourself?" I asked.

"In a word, yes," he said. "I give you guys enough shit. I expect to get plenty of it back." He didn't look too worried about that happening. He was a big boy, he could deal with it.

"I decided to be nice." I kissed him back. It was nice to do that, especially given the fiery start to our relationship. "Don't worry, I'll think of something sarcastic to say soon."

"I wouldn't have it any other way." He touched his forehead to mine in a gesture that was surprisingly intimate and sweet. Sometimes, it was difficult to figure Beau Pennington out. I liked that. He always kept me guessing.

Zeke pulled the microphone out from its stand and turned it on. "All right ladies and gentlemen, boys and girls, are you ready to rock out, Paris?"

"Let's do it," Landon called out. He had the strap of his bass around his neck and a grin on his face.

I couldn't help smiling in response. He had a particularly contagious smile. The fact he still managed to do it after what he told me about his mother was even more miraculous. The more I learnt about these guys, the more I was amazed and besotted. How could anyone not fall head over heels in love with them?

I had, and I was loving every minute of it.

I grooved along with the guys as they started to play. It was only a sound check, but the guys held nothing back. That, of course, was why they were so successful. They put their hearts and souls into each performance and their fans, and I, loved them for it.

As I listened and enjoyed the performance, I couldn't help but dwell on what Landon told me about his mother. I understood now why it took longer for him to gravitate towards me, even when he was attracted. As well as his deep involvement with Channing, he must have assumed I would walk away, like so many other people in his life had. I had no intention of doing that. Not if I could help it.

I had a feeling I was going to have to prove that to him.

6

LANDON

"So, you told Abbie about your childhood?" Channing asked softly. "How did she take it?" He sounded worried about me.

He was sweet that way, always putting my needs first and looking out for me. He'd been like that since we met. We clicked immediately, but like with Abbie, I held back, scared he'd walk right out of my life as quickly as he'd walked in. Equally scared he realised he was too good for a guy like me.

By some kind of miracle, he stuck around, the one solid island in a sea of crazy. I loved him for it.

"As well as I expected." I nestled against my boyfriend's chest and debated leaning over to steal some of his croissant. I'd eaten mine already while he only picked at his. "She's sweet. I didn't think she would freak out. Especially knowing about the rest of the guys and their shit. Mine was pretty mild in comparison."

I hated feeling sorry for myself or making a fuss. Yeah, I went through shit, but other people went through worse.

"Hey." Channing caught my chin between his thumb and forefinger and turned my face towards him. "No one deserves to go through the stuff you did. Especially you. Breaks my heart to think about it." His gorgeous hazel eyes showed the truth of his words. He'd probably hide me away in a blanket fort if he could. With beer and too much cheese, if there was such a thing.

"Yours wasn't a bed of roses either," I pointed out. "Luckily, we both turned out okay. More or less."

Still gripping my chin, he kissed me. "We both turned out perfectly weird. That's the best way to be." He let my chin go and pushed his plate over to me. "I saw you eying it off. Might as well finish it. I'm not going to."

"You're the best," I told him.

He sat back to sip his coffee. "Hell yeah, I am. I'd tell you not to forget it, but there's no way you would. I'm that fuckin' epic." He tipped his head to the side and smiled.

"Yes you are," I said before biting into the croissant. "I swear they taste better here than anywhere else in the world."

"Everything tastes better in France than anywhere else in the world, because we're eating it here. Even greasy takeaway burgers."

"To be fair, greasy takeaway burgers taste good everywhere," I said. I tried to stick to a healthy diet, but once in a while I couldn't resist the lure of a good burger. They were like a siren, calling to me, begging me to stuff my face. Luring me with their delicious meaty juices…

Okay, I didn't need that much convincing. One of the guys suggests burgers and the rest of us follow along. We were super good at enabling each other when it came to food, music and sex.

Not necessarily in that order.

"You're not wrong, Lan," Channing said. He was the only one who called me that. Just like I was the only one who called him Chan.

Our fans called us Lanning or sometimes Chandon, which was super cute.

What would they call us if we both got together with Abbie? Whatever it was, I already couldn't pronounce it.

"Did you tell Abbie everything?" Channing put

down his coffee cup and looked at me like he already knew the answer.

"Not everything," I admitted. "Not about that last time I saw Mum. It...kinda stings still. Y'know? I just wanted her to be happy for me." Even more, I wanted Mum to get her shit together. If I could, I would have dragged her off to rehab and made them lock her in until she wasn't a danger to herself. Or anyone else.

"Yeah, I know." He draped an arm over my shoulders. "At least my parents were just as shitty about it."

"Not surprising, given their strong views on LGBT folk," I said regretfully. His were the dictionary definition of homophobic. If conversion therapy was legal, they would have forced him to do it. Correction, they would have tried. Channing would have told them to fuck off.

"After everything my mother did, you think she'd be more understanding. The shit she did..." I hadn't expected her to be so harsh. So—bitter.

The worst part was, I didn't think she'd mind if I was gay, but somehow, for some reason I couldn't grasp, my being bi was offensive to her. It wasn't the first time I encountered shitty attitudes like that, but from my own mother...

At the end of the day, the best thing I could do

would be not to sweat it too much. Her attitude, her words, they weren't going to change who I was, even if I wanted them to. Which I didn't.

I was attracted to who I was attracted to. End of story.

"She'll get over it," Channing said. "And if she doesn't, you have the rest of us. Forever." He lightly touched his nose to mine. "You know I love you, right?"

"Not as much as I love you," I said. That was our thing we said to each other. Our version of, 'I love you more.' "I don't know what I would do without you."

"Lucky for you, you'll never have to find out." He wiggled his nose against mine. "I'm not going anywhere."

"I don't think Abbie is either," I said carefully. "How do you feel about that?"

We talked about her lots of times in the last few months, but I always felt the need to check back in case his feelings changed. As busy as we were, it was easy to get caught up in everything and forget to communicate. The last thing I wanted was to lose anyone I loved because I hadn't taken the time.

Yeah, I was insecure as shit, but I had good reason to be.

"I feel the same way you feel," Channing said easily. "The same way the rest of the guys feel. There's something about her that draws us all in like a magnet. She just… Belongs. Like you and I belong."

I nodded, relieved to hear him say that. "You're right, that is exactly how I feel. But I worry about after the tour. How are things going to work then?"

"I don't know," he admitted. "But I know they will work out because we want them to. We'll do whatever it takes to make it happen. Right?" His expression was intense. He wanted Abbie as much as I did. As much as we wanted each other.

"Yeah, we will," I agreed. "Things are going to work out. I can feel it." I kissed him and then finished off the rest of the croissant while looking around the small café.

The rest of Wolf Venom, Blazing Violet and a bunch of tour staff sat finishing breakfast. Only a couple of people who sat at a table near the window had nothing to do with us. We'd pretty much taken over the whole place this morning. The café workers didn't seem to mind. Most of us were on our second cups of coffee.

My gaze was drawn over to where Abbie sat with Zeke, Asher and Violet, the lead singer of Blazing Violet. Violet's hair was as bright as mine, but purple rather than blue. She and Abbie seem to have formed a friendship during the tour. If she got sick of being surrounded by us guys, she had someone to talk to.

I couldn't not support that.

Abbie smiled and laughed at something Asher said.

I knew she had absolutely no idea how fucking gorgeous she was. Not just beautiful. Channing used the right word—magnetic. I wanted to look at her for hours on end. I wanted to listen to her talk and sing and laugh.

I wanted to touch her and fuck her like I had the other night. I wanted to curl up in a big bed with her and Channing and stay there for a year or ten. Maybe we could get the other guys to bring us essentials like coffee and croissants. That didn't seem like too much to ask.

Okay, they might get sick of that after the first year or two. They could just join us. A cuddle puddle for seven sounded perfect to me. With a huge movie screen at one end and shelves full of toys and rope at the other.

Channing handed me a napkin.

"What's that for?" I took it and frowned at him.

"For wiping up the drool on your chin." He

grinned. "If you stare at her any longer, you're gonna start salivating."

I felt my face heat. "I stare at you just as much," I insisted. Was he teasing or jealous? I didn't want him to be jealous. I didn't want anything to mess up our relationship.

"You're adorable when you blush." He touched my nose with the tip of his finger, and traced the line up to my forehead and around the side of my face to my chin. "Even your ears turn red."

"I'm adorable all the time," I protested. "Just like you." I tilted my head so I could kiss the heel of his hand.

"Just like Abbie," Channing said. "I can't stop thinking about both of you the other night. It was pretty fucking epic."

"It was." We'd shared partners often enough to be in sync for much of the time. I knew a lot of them thought it was strange, but it made perfect sense to us. With Abbie, though, it was different. I felt like the three of us were extensions of each other. Like we all knew what was in each other's heads and what we all liked.

Granted, we'd watched her with the other guys a few times, and took mental notes, but doing it was a different story.

"What do you think she would think of..." I leaned over to whisper in his ear.

"I think she'd like it," Channing said, a glint in his eye. "I know I would. She seems game to try anything, as long as we're respectful and shit."

"We're always respectful and shit," I said with a nod.

Channing chuckled. "Yeah, we are. We're good dudes."

"The best." After a moment I added, "The best of the best." Our bandmates were pretty good dudes too. Most of the time. We were lucky to have found them. Even luckier to have had the success we had.

Okay, there was a shit load of hard work involved too, and a fuck ton of talent, but also some luck.

"Anyone would think we have healthy egos or something," Channing said with a laugh.

I snorted. "Pfft, not us. We're as humble as... I dunno what. Something fucking humble."

Okay, we weren't, but I'd met a lot of people worse than us. Some with good reason, others not so much. There was nothing wrong with having a good opinion of yourself, as long as you weren't a dick about it.

Channing's gaze fixed on something outside the window. He blinked and then frowned.

"What?" I turned and squinted, trying to figure out what caught his attention.

He shook his head slowly, then tore his eyes off the window. "It's nothing. I thought I saw someone I knew, that's all."

"You're in a café in Paris, which is, at this very moment, full of people you know," I pointed out. "And this isn't all of us. Was it someone from the tour?"

"No." He peered into his coffee cup like he wished it was still full and hot. "It's nothing. They just looked familiar, that's all. Nothing to worry about."

"Okay," I said slowly. I wanted to believe him, but he looked rattled. Then again, a lot of things got him rattled. Never for very long, but enough to be noticeable and to make me worry each time. I would never not worry about him if anything bothered him. No matter how big or small a thing might be.

"Do you want another coffee?" I asked.

"What I'd really like is to run all the way up the Eiffel Tower," he said, snapping back to his normal self again. "That would get the blood pumping."

"If anyone I know would, or could, do that, it would be you," I told him.

Him or Penn. They were both bundles of pent up energy that needed somewhere to go. "Maybe you should challenge Penn to a race up to the second floor."

He looked thoughtful. "I wonder if we could get Levi to convince them to let us race all the way to the top."

The stairs from the second floor to the top of the Eiffel Tower weren't open to the public. But we were Wolf Venom. Would they bend the rules for us?

"I would bet on you," I told him. Even if I didn't think he would win, I would still put my money on Channing. As much as I loved Penn, Channing was my person. I would support him no matter what he did.

He smiled, but he still looked troubled.

7

ABBIE

"ARE THEY REALLY GONNA DO THIS?" I slipped on my sunglasses against the glare of the sun and straightened my black ball cap. Okay, Asher's cap, but I swiped it a few days ago and he hadn't said anything.

Jackson glanced down at me and shrugged. He had his 'long-suffering manager' expression in place. "It can't hurt. Well, it shouldn't hurt us. It might hurt them when they're doing it, but if they're that silly, who am I to stop them?"

Because of tourists and safety concerns, Channing and Penn weren't allowed to race up the Eiffel Tower. Much to their disappointment and a non-zero level of swearing. Being the guys they were, once the challenge was on, they had to follow through. Because—of course they did.

They'd hunted for somewhere else ever since. They finally decided to race each other around the outside of the Olympiastadion in Munich.

It was as good a place as any, I supposed.

"Just another day in the life of Wolf Venom," Asher said lightly. He pulled his navy blue cap down to shade his eyes better. Like all the guys, he wore designer sunglasses. Mine were just a cheap pair I picked up in Sydney airport. It might be time for me to upgrade.

"Another day in the life of Channing and Penn," Landon agreed, nodding. He didn't wear a cap, just sunglasses with big rims, shorts and a singlet that showed off his muscular arms and tattoos. The arm holes were so wide, when he lifted his arms, his nipple ring glinted in the sunlight.

"I didn't realise they were so competitive with each other," I said. Of course, you didn't achieve a high level of success without a decent amount of mongrel in you, as they say. Determination, fight, whatever you wanted to call it.

"It's not that they're competitive with each other," Zeke said slowly. He was dressed from head to toe in black, including a cap the same as mine.

"It's that they're competitive with *everyone*," Tully finished for him. "They both came from families of overachievers that expected them to be over-overachievers. Sometimes they like to rebel against their upbringing and sometimes they go along with it."

"And sometimes they like to be seen," Landon said. The crowd had already noticed us and started to gather, wondering what the hell we were doing.

"They're going to be seen all right," I said. I couldn't miss the paparazzi mingling with the crowd. They'd already taken several photos of us. Unfortunately for them, we weren't doing anything embarrassing or scandalous.

Yet. Give it a minute, that could change.

"Am I the only one resisting the urge to flip the paparazzi the finger?" Asher asked cheerfully.

"Nope, I'm resisting too," Zeke said.

"I was thinking about mooning them." Landon stepped closer to me, until his bare arm brushed mine.

I laced my fingers in his. I sensed he liked to have someone physically close by as much as possible. Part of constantly thinking people will leave you included struggling to let them out of your sight. Channing wasn't just his boyfriend, he was his emotional support saxophonist. Didn't everyone need one of those?

He squeezed my hand and I caught the look of gratitude on his face.

"You're not really thinking of mooning anyone are you?" I asked him.

"I would say not in public, but we both know I would." He grinned. "Not in front of paparazzi though. The whole world isn't ready to see my ass." He spoke with no hint of modesty. He'd probably run around naked and not blink an eye.

Why not, his ass was adorable.

"They aren't ready to see mine either," I agreed. There was exhibitionism and then there was getting yourself arrested for public nudity. Not to mention having photos of you go viral. It was a fine line.

"Let's save both for later," he suggested.

"Deal," I said. My stomach fluttered. I doubted there would come a day when I didn't want any of the guys. Or all of them. Part of me still wondered if that was greedy, but most of me didn't care if it was.

Before I met the guys, I wouldn't have dreamt about dating any of them. They were so far out of my league we weren't on the same planet. Now, a whole freaking rock band was mine. Six guys. It was surreal and magical. Whichever direction I turned, there was a guy who cared about me. Who I cared about.

I was beyond blessed, and grateful for every moment of it.

"Looks like they're ready," Jackson said.

Levi, who stood about ten metres away, raised his arm above his head. He'd travelled around with us since Dublin. Penn joked he'd stuck around just for this. Levi hadn't denied it.

"Ready. Set," Levi said loudly.

Channing and Penn jostled each other playfully, trying to put each other off. Or knock each other over.

"Remember," Levi called out, obviously trying to catch them off guard so one or both would break early. "No tripping each other, no trying to hurt each other, and no running into members of the public."

He didn't say anything about not running into paparazzi. That probably went without saying.

"Go!" Levi shouted. He dropped his arm and took a few hurried steps back as the guys leapt forward at a run, Penn slightly ahead due to having a height advantage.

The crowd, who cottoned on to what was going on by now, started to cheer.

It's not every day you get impromptu entertainment from a pair of rock gods. Especially hot ones who were going to be glistening with sweat by the end of this race.

Yum.

"They're going to need to shower after this," Landon remarked.

"You're right," I said. "I wonder if they'll need any help."

"Only the winner," he said with a sly smile.

"You're sure Channing will win, aren't you?" I asked.

I didn't think he'd help Penn shower, nor would the keyboardist want him to. Was it wrong that I pictured that anyway and liked what I saw?

No, I decided, it wasn't. Luckily I had plenty more fantasies to live out, and guys happy to help me fulfill them.

"He's quick," Landon said. "He's built more for running than Penn is."

"Penn used to run in school," Asher said. "If half of what he says is true, he was good at it. When his parents let him take part." The grimace on his lips showed what he thought about that.

"I guess we'll see," Zeke said. His expression matched Asher's. I suspected the Brantley family was as supportive as Penn's when it came to having fun.

I swung my gaze away the direction Penn and Channing went, but they'd already run out of sight.

"What if it's a tie?" I asked.

"The hotel has a big shower," Landon said without hesitation. He looked over at me and grinned, then leaned in to lightly kiss my mouth.

"We could all fit," Asher said. "Even Jackson."

The band's manager looked at him in surprise, then shook his head and looked away.

"I think that's a no," Zeke remarked.

Jackson didn't look back when he said, "That's a fuck no. You guys are enough trouble without going that far."

"You know you love us," Asher said. He pouted playfully at Jackson's back.

"You're okay," Jackson said patiently. "Doesn't mean I want to get naked with you all."

"Which one of us do you want to get naked with?" Tully asked teasingly.

Jackson sighed. When Levi walked over to join us, he said, "I think I should get a pay raise for having to put up with these guys' apparent fascination with my sex life."

Levi laughed. "If they're hassling you, they're leaving me alone."

"That doesn't seem fair," Asher said. "Fortunately,

we have the ability to hassle you both. We're equal opportunity hasslers."

I smiled at the infectious grin on Asher's face. The whole vibe from White Wolf Records was so different to what I experienced at Onyx Riot. Everyone genuinely seemed to like each other. To say we were one big family was usually such a cliché, but in this case it was true.

Jackson and Levi were like big brothers or uncles to everyone else, rather than bosses and managers. Most bosses wouldn't let the guys get away with half the things they did, for a start.

"Levi, what were you saying about getting a drum machine?" One side of Jackson's mouth pulled up in a smile.

"I believe I said it would be cheaper and less trouble than Asher." Levi grinned.

"Hey!" Asher said in protest. "You wouldn't replace me. No drum machine could sound as good, or look as awesome, as I do." He didn't even look slightly concerned that they might follow through with the threat.

"I dunno." Jackson scratched the side of his head. "Technology has come a long way." He lost the struggle to hold back a smile.

"Fine, I'll stop hassling you. For now." Asher

crossed his arms over his chest, stuck out his chin and looked at Jackson down his nose. He was too stinking cute when he was pretending to be serious.

"No doubt that will last about an hour," Jackson said dryly, clearly unmoved.

"An hour if you're lucky," Asher agreed. He craned his neck. "Any sign of them yet? How long does it take to run around one stadium?"

"It depends on the stadium, but more than five minutes, babe," Zeke told him. "Although, knowing them, they probably stopped for a latte." He gestured in the general direction of the other side of the stadium.

"If there's a place that sells coffee on the other side of the stadium," Tully said slowly, a frown on his brow, "then why are we standing here?"

"That's a good question," Asher said. "It's probably because we'd get distracted by the coffee and forget to watch the race."

"There's a race?" Zeke asked jokingly.

Asher turned to him. "So I've heard. I'm not sure if the rumour is accurate or not though." He rubbed his chin as though deep in thought.

"I think you missed your calling," Jackson said. "You all should have been stand-up comedians." He gave a playful half roll of his eyes.

"I think that's a backhanded way of saying we're fucking hilarious," Zeke said.

"That's what it sounded like to me," Tully agreed. "Thanks, Jackson."

Jackson snorted. "You're welcome. I think." He scrunched up his face and shook his head.

Asher hooked an arm through Jackson's. "Aren't you lucky to have the best job in the world? Imagine how many people wish they could hang around with us all day, everyday. You're basically living the dream right here."

"Lucky me," Jackson said ironically. In spite of his apparent lack of enthusiasm, he smiled. "Yeah, okay. I am fortunate to do what I do. There are definitely bands out there who are a lot worse than you guys."

"Like who?" Asher asked. His face lit up with curiosity.

"I would tell you, but I signed an NDA saying I wouldn't," Jackson said.

Asher groaned. "Fucking NDAs. They spoil all the fun."

"They also stop me from spilling all your secrets," Jackson pointed out.

"Awesome NDAs," Asher said, snapping his fingers. "They're the best thing since sliced bread."

"I've never seen you change your tune that quickly," Tully teased. "Even on stage."

Asher laughed. "Yeah, well, when you're wrong, you're wrong. Although, I bet sometimes Jackson would like to get shit off his chest." He gave the manager a cagey look.

"That's why Jax talks to me about stuff," Levi said. "You're not allowed to know things, but I am. You know, being the boss and all."

Asher turned and cocked his head at Tully. "Tull, if we signed with your label, would you tell us stuff?"

"Nope," Tully said lightly. "Not if there's an NDA in place. Which there would be. Besides, everything we do is more interesting anyway. Probably." He raised his hands to either side like he wasn't sure.

"Exactly," Jackson said. "If I told you, you'd be bored silly, instead of just the regular kind of silly."

Before Asher could respond, a ripple of excitement passed through the crowd. People started to chant either Channing's name or Penn's. It seemed like they had an equal amount of fans amongst those watching.

Landon squeezed my hand hard with excitement. He was standing on his toes and craning his neck to see over the crowd.

I didn't even try. If he couldn't see, I had no chance.

Not until Zeke said, "Want a piggyback?"

I barely had time to register what he said before the guys were helping me up to sit on Zeke's shoulders. I gripped on tight with my legs, feet hooked around each other, his hands holding mine.

"Are you sure this is okay?" I asked. Was that him wobbling or me? Or both?

"You barely weigh a thing," Zeke said. He was definitely not the one wobbling. "I could have you sit on me all day."

I snorted a laugh. "I bet you could." And not on his shoulders either.

"How's the view up there?" Tully asked.

I looked around. "Amazing. I can see the guys. They're neck and neck." Until I saw them, I hadn't realised how nervous I was to let them out of my sight. Security surrounded the stadium, blending in with the crowds, but I still liked them where I could see them.

I let go of one of Zeke's hands long enough to wave at a paparazzo as he started to snap photos of us. This was the kind of positive story I didn't mind them sharing with the world. Nothing scandalous, just sitting on the shoulders of one of my boyfriends.

"Where's the finish line?" I asked.

"Oh, shit." While we snickered, Levi trotted back over to where he'd started the race. He must have forgotten to get back into position until I reminded him.

He got back in place just in time to drop his arm and celebrate the winner.

8

ABBIE

"That was awesome." Now we were inside the stadium and away from public scrutiny, it was safe to push myself up on my toes and kiss Penn.

"Of course it was." He snaked an arm around my waist and pulled me until my breasts were pressed against his firm chest. "I won."

"And we're never going to hear the end of it, are we?" I teased.

"Nope." He slanted his mouth over mine and kissed me, rough and demanding. "What do I get for winning?"

"Bragging rights," Levi said as he slid past us in the stadium corridor.

"The promise of a rematch." Channing was close behind Levi, his hand in Landon's. He was still smiling. He might be as competitive as fuck, but he was a good loser. Probably because he knew there would be chances to beat Penn another day.

"Any time, dude," Penn said. "I'll wipe the floor with you again."

"You didn't win by that much," Asher pointed out.

"I'll take you on too," Penn told him. "You don't get to criticise if you won't put your money where your mouth is."

"That is a really weird expression," Asher said. He shrugged and hurried after Zeke as the lead singer disappeared into the stadium's green room.

"He's right, it is," Tully said. "Personally, I'd love to see who would win a race between you and Asher."

Penn drew himself up a little taller. "Me. Asher is too busy running his mouth off to outrun me."

Asher stuck his head out of the green room door. "I heard that." He ducked back inside.

Penn snorted a laugh. "I need a shower." He eyed me speculatively.

I looked back at him. In the corner of my eye, I saw Channing and Landon. They seemed to be having the same conversation.

"There's plenty of showers for everyone," I said.

"Good, because I wasn't asking." Penn took my

hand and led me through the green room, to the bathrooms at the back.

All of our things were here already, including changes of clothes. I fully intended to have a shower anyway, but why not share? We might even take a moment to get clean.

"Of course you weren't." I gave him a long look before heading into one of the cubicles.

"We could conserve water by sharing," Landon pointed out.

"It would definitely be good for the planet if all four of us were in there." Channing nodded.

When he put it that way…

Penn shrugged and reached down with one hand to pull his shirt off over his head. "There's plenty of room."

There wasn't really, but that was kind of the point.

Faint heat in my face, and with the full knowledge all three guys were watching me, I started to shed my clothes.

Funny that, even after fucking in a room full of strangers, I was still self-conscious about my body. Less than I used to be, thanks to six guys who always seemed to like what they saw.

"You are so fucking gorgeous," Penn whispered.

He waved to the other guys in and closed and locked the door behind him.

"I know you are," I told him. He was mouthwateringly hot as fuck.

Since fair's fair, I watched them strip off, until I was surrounded by naked, sweaty muscle.

Holy fucking yes please.

Penn turned the water on and kept his hand under it until steam started to rise. He nodded to himself, then grabbed my wrists and turned me around to face the shower wall. He pinned me to the tiles with one hand.

Water gushed down my hair and down my back, hot, but not as hot as Penn pressing the full length of his body against me so the shower poured down over us both. His cock poked into the back of my leg, hard and ready.

He ground against my thigh, his breath a ragged groan over the water.

"So fucking gorgeous," he muttered. With one hand keeping me in place, he reached around with the other, deft fingers nudging my thighs open and delving into my clit and folds.

I moved my feet further apart, giving him better access. He grunted in triumph as he found my clit and traced circles around and over it with two fingers.

I blinked water out of my eyes and turned so my sodden hair fell off my face.

Landon was on his knees right beside me. His fingers were cupped around Channing's balls, the saxophonist's cock right in front of him, thick and firm.

Landon ran his fingers up and over Channing's balls a few times, while teasingly flicking his tongue at his tip.

Channing groaned and looked ready to slam himself into Landon's mouth. Teasing must be their thing, because he waited until Landon was ready to slip his lips over him and started to suck. Then he curled his fingers in Landon's blue hair and pulled him closer, going deeper.

Forever, I'd always find that arousing as fuck. Muscular, masculine men being intimate. All the smokin' hot.

"You want to do that too?" Penn asked, his tone rough with desire, mouth right beside my ear.

He loosened his grip on my wrists. "Get on your knees." He pushed me down so I was half in, half out of the water, kneeling beside Landon. He tangled his fingers in my hair and positioned his cock in front of my mouth.

"What do you say?" He smirked at me.

"Yes, sir." Eagerly, I opened to let him slide between my lips.

I sucked him hard, using my lips and tongue, taking him all the way to the back of my throat while I cupped and stroked his balls with my hand.

He thrust into me a few times, then pulled my head back and guided me over to Channing's cock.

Landon sat back on his heels, eyes dark with desire while he watched me suck his boyfriend.

I watched him back, our eyes locked on each other.

After a minute or two, Landon rose and stood where the spray from the shower landed in droplets on his tanned skin.

Penn drew me back off Channing's cock and guided me over to Landon's.

"Fuck yeah," Landon breathed as I closed my lips around his hot length.

I teased his weeping slit with the tip of my tongue and sucked, my eyes still on his.

Penn muttered something incoherent and drew me back to him.

Landon crouched back down between me and

Channing. He teased Channing's cock with his mouth, while stretching around my ass and running his fingers lightly over and around my pussy.

"You're so wet," he said. "Not just from the shower."

I laughed and tried not to get a mouthful of water. Of course I was wet. Between his touch and Penn alternating my mouth between his cock and Channing's, I was a matter of breaths away from coming.

When Landon swivelled my hips around and pulled me down onto his cock, I almost did. My whole body tingled with a surge of blood and passion.

Only Penn's barked order, "Don't come yet," stopped me from exploding then and there.

I groaned and looked up at him in playful defiance.

He gave me an arched eyebrow and a, 'Don't you fucking dare,' look.

With my eyes, I told him how much he sucked, but he smirked and kept on being smug. He knew I'd wait until he told me to come, whatever it took.

As if in on the game, Landon thrust into me slowly, taking his time, while he gave Channing's cock the same careful treatment.

What else could I do but join in? I slid my mouth off Penn's length and teased him lightly with the tip of my tongue.

He gave me an amused look, but I just smiled.

Takes four to play this game, buddy.

Finally, on some unseen signal, we all moved faster, sucked harder, thrust deeper. We went from languid to frantic in a heartbeat.

Channing was the first to come, his hands wrapped around the back of Landon's wet hair. His hips swung back and forth as he milked himself dry between the bassist's lips.

So. Fucking. Hot.

He slid his softened length out of Landon's mouth and sat on the tiles beside me. While Landon thrust hungrily, Channing's fingers hummed against my clit, barely touching at first, then firmer, as if searching for my orgasm.

Concentration on his face, he slipped past my folds and into me, so two of his fingers and Landon's cock were inside my pussy at the same time.

My eyes widened. That was... different, but I liked it.

They set a rhythm of pressing up into me, both relentless, as if wanting me to come to spite Penn.

At the same time, Penn's eyes were on me, ordering me to wait.

Blood roared through me, pushing me closer and closer.

Landon kept a hand on my hip and reached around to tease my nipple with the other.

I gasped around Penn's cock. I needed to come so badly it was almost an exquisite agony.

I turned pleading eyes up at Penn.

He hesitated for a moment longer, then nodded. "Okay, you've been a good girl for long enough. Come like a dirty whore."

On command, my whole body exploded with pleasure. I might have cried out and bit down on Penn's cock. He jumped, but didn't pull out. Instead, he came too, thrusting and grunting while water and orgasmic goodness washed down over me.

My juices gushed over Landon's cock and Channing's fingers, driving an orgasm out of Landon. He thrust harder, deeper, furious, gasping and moaning until the last delicious drop of pleasure was forced out of us both.

I pulled off Penn's cock, swallowed, then flopped down under the hot flow of water and let it wash me clean.

9

LANDON

"HEY, I need to talk to you about something." I curled my fingers around Abbie's wrist and stopped her from taking more than a couple of steps from the tour bus.

I'd thought about this the whole way from Munich to Zürich. I could have talked to her on the drive, but the moment hadn't come. The mood was light the whole way. I didn't want to be the one to shatter it.

Now, I couldn't keep it in any longer. Shit, I was freaking out on the inside. On the outside too, judging by her expression. I was trying to play it cool. Seems I didn't pull it off.

Fuck.

"That sounds serious," she said, her tone deceptively light. She looked worried, scared even.

I should have thought this through better before I spoke. She always seemed so strong and confident, sometimes I forgot what she'd been through with Vance and Pete, and the assholes from the press.

"Shit," I said softly. I pulled her to me and kissed her nose. "It's nothing like that, honey, I promise."

I grabbed Channing's hand in my free one and laced my fingers in Abbie's. We walked slowly behind the others towards the door that led inside Letzigrund Stadion.

"What is it about?" she asked. In spite of my assurances, she looked like she thought I was about to break up with her.

I was never very good at this stuff. The other guys had the charisma, the way with words. I was awkward as hell.

I exchanged glances with Channing. He nodded reassuringly and smiled. At least one of us had faith in me.

I swallowed down my nerves, part of them anyway, and spoke. "It's about my mother."

"Have you heard from her?" Abbie asked immediately. "Is she okay?" Of course she would be concerned and interested. I called her honey, but she was sweeter than that.

I shook my head. "I don't know. I just wanted to tell you about the last time I saw her. We had a fight. She…" I glanced at Channing again. "She wasn't accepting of him and I. She didn't understand how I could be into guys and girls. She…"

I felt like I was picking at my own scab with this. Opening wounds which were still healing.

I swallowed, then spat out the words, "She told me she wished she hadn't had me." That was the tip of the iceberg, but it was the main point.

Abbie winced and drew me to a stop. "I'm sure she didn't mean that."

"I'm sure she did," I said with equal conviction. It wasn't just the words, it was the truth behind them. More than once, the guys whom she was with wanted her to ditch me. Then they'd ditched her. She made me feel like a dead weight around her shoulders. The thing keeping her from living her life, or giving in and dying in the gutter.

She made me wish she'd never had me too.

"She was harsh," Channing said simply. "It's up to him, of course, I'll support him no matter what, but I'd be happy if he never saw her again. He deserves better."

He looked furious now as he had back then, six months ago. At the time, I thought he'd punch Mum out. If she was a man, he probably would have.

"Yeah," I said softly. "Channing was amazing." I gave him a soft look, trying to convey the love I felt for him. "He let me cry on his shoulder for about three days."

Okay, that was an exaggeration. It was two and half days.

After everything she put me through, the last thing I wanted to hear, needed to hear, was that she never wanted me in the first place. I shouted back at her that I'd never asked to be born and things went downhill from there. The things we said to each other...

I wasn't sure if I'd ever get a chance to make amends.

Or even if I wanted to.

No, that's not true, I definitely wanted to, if only for my own peace of mind.

"Anyway," I continued, "Mum and I didn't part on good terms. It was ugly as shit. I'm sorry to dump all of this on you, I needed you to know the whole story." I didn't want to hold back anything from her. It was why I needed to tell her about that fight. It was a small deal in the scheme of things, especially compared with what she'd been through, but it was a big deal for me. My mother made letting me down an art form. I didn't want to do the same to the people I loved. I needed Abbie to know that. I was all in. This was my roundabout way of telling her that.

"Thanks for telling me," Abbie said softly. "There's nothing you could ever say to me that would make me turn my back on you like that. Either of you."

"You say that," I said, "but you don't know *all* our dirty little secrets." I managed a faint smile. Just most of them.

She smiled back and squeezed my hand. "There's nothing so dirty…or so little, that would make me run away." She grimaced. "I mean, you know I did some dumb things and none of you turned your back on me. That goes both ways. Always. Okay?"

"None of us has to worry about *little*." My smile got bigger and more genuine now.

"That's true," she said. "Little is definitely not a word I would use to describe any of you."

I swung their hands to either side of me while we walked. I could get used to this. Not just being able to open up to her, not just being with them, but the whole feeling of belonging.

In the back of my mind was still the thought she

might walk away and break my heart. For the most part, I was able to ignore it, but it lingered.

Why would a woman like her want a guy like me anyway? Especially when she had five others to choose from? Not to mention a planet full of single guys who would probably do just about anything to get her.

I was sure she didn't even notice the stares she got when she walked down the street. It wasn't just because she was famous, or because she was surrounded by six hot guys. People looked at *her*. I looked at her a lot too. Some days, it was hard to tear my eyes away from both of them.

Insecure Landon, who sat on my shoulder like a dead weight, told me they were both too good for me. That they might hook up and run away together. That at the end, I'd be the one to end up alone. That—

Fuck off, I told him. *Let me enjoy myself. If shit goes down, I'll deal with it.* Even if they ripped out my heart.

"Don't look now," Channing said suddenly. "We have company." He nodded straight ahead.

I turned to look. Not surprising, a gaggle of paparazzi, cameras and phones in hand, waited outside the entrance to the arena.

"Want me to let your hand go?" I asked Abbie. Photos of her sitting on Zeke's shoulders went viral and fans seemed to love it. To then see her holding hands with me might confuse the issue.

She hesitated for a moment. "Not if you don't want to," she said finally. "Let them think whatever they want to think. It's not like they're wrong anyway. Relationships like ours are more normal than people seem to think. Maybe we can help to normalise it a bit more. It's way past time people stopped stigmatising polyamorous relationships."

"I couldn't agree more." I nodded and walked a bit more proudly. She wasn't just gorgeous and sweet, she was a badass.

I hoped she didn't end up regretting the choice. We all knew how vicious the paparazzi could be. A shiver of worry crept up my spine. What if they were so vicious she changed her mind and walked away from us?

Yeah, that was insecure Landon again. He didn't know when to piss off. Asshole.

I thought about letting her hand go anyway, but I didn't. I couldn't seem to make myself do it. The little boy in me who just wanted to hug his mother, wanted to hold on to her and Channing and never let either of them go.

Yeah, even big, bad rock stars have inner little boys and insecure assholes messing with their heads.

As soon as we got close enough, the paparazzi started to take photos. People stopped to stare and point when they realised who we were.

Lines and lines of people wound around barricades outside the stadium. By the look of it, a lot of them camped out overnight just to get a front row spot at the concert tonight. Sweet. I loved their dedication. It went a long way to bolstering my ego.

We waved, but the paparazzi stepped in front of the crowds to take photos.

"Get the fuck out of the way," one of the fans shouted.

"Yeah, leave them alone," shouted another.

Someone in the crowd started to chant and everyone else quickly took it up. "Wolf Venom! Wolf Venom! Venom! Venom! Venom!"

They started to push against the barricades. Security, dressed in black uniforms with radios on their shoulders, hurried in from all angles to hold them back.

"Let's get inside," Jackson said, urgency in his tone. "Before things get ugly."

The crowd shouted louder, more demanding.

Someone threw a water bottle. It slammed into the shoulder of one of the paparazzi.

The crowd cheered and jeered, pushed harder against the flimsy barricades.

Security waded through the crowds, trying to reach the person who threw the bottle. The fans immediately closed rank around them.

"Shit, this isn't how this is supposed to go," Abbie said. Her face was pale. Her hand was sweaty in mine.

I murmured my agreement and pulled her and Channing along a little faster. The sooner we got out of the area, the less chance there would be of a riot, or something else, happening.

That was the last thing we needed this close to the end of the European leg of the tour. Okay, that and a bunch of other shit that might happen. Fuck knows we'd been through enough already.

We were herded along, but I kept looking over my shoulder. I couldn't tell if they got the person who threw the bottle but I caught Abbie's expression in the corner of my eye. She was white as snow, her mouth pressed in a tight line.

I didn't need to be a mind reader to know what she was thinking. She was remembering the music festival in Queensland where someone threw a can and hit her in the face. A bunch of other people had thrown cans and water bottles onto the stage as well.

I had to grab Channing's hand to keep him from jumping down into the audience and start swinging. All of the guys were pissed, but him most of all.

Honestly, if he'd thrown a few punches, I would have joined him.

And we'd be locked up in jail right now instead of hurrying into the stadium in Zürich.

"Are you okay?" I knew she'd been asked that at least three hundred million times in the last few months, but I couldn't help asking again.

"Um, kinda," she said. "Just a little freaked out. I'm not a fan of when people start throwing things. Especially when they actually hit people with them."

I let go of her hand and slipped an arm around her instead. "Me either. At least they're not throwing things at us this time."

"Right, but that guy could have been badly hurt." She looked back over her shoulder as we hurried through the doorway.

"Only you would feel bad for paparazzi after what they've done to you," I told her.

She looked up at me and smiled. "I only hold a grudge against some paparazzi in particular, not them as a group."

"You're crazy," Penn said. "They all fucking suck. Not in a good way either."

"If they sucked in a good way, would you want them to?" Asher asked. He seemed genuinely curious, but grinned teasingly at the same time.

"Hell no." Penn grimaced. "Being an asshole might be contagious. I don't want to catch it." After a moment he added, "I'm enough of an asshole already. But at least I am a faster runner than Channing." He smiled slyly at the saxophonist.

Channing flipped him off. "I had an off day, that's all. Next time, I'm going to whip your ass." He rubbed the palms of his hands together like he couldn't wait to get on with the job.

"Promises, promises," Penn said. "Maybe I don't want to race you again after all. Gotta keep my reputation intact."

"If you don't race me again, you'll get a reputation as a chicken," Channing challenged.

"I don't have a problem with that," Penn said lightly. "But I'm going to race you again to prove that I can beat you again. But next time, let's have higher stakes."

"Like what?" Channing asked.

Penn shrugged. "I dunno. I'll think of something."

"Whatever it is, game on," Channing said. "I look forward to you eating my dust."

"At least it's never boring around here," I said to Abbie.

She snorted a laugh. "It certainly isn't." She was a tad less pale, but still clearly rattled.

I hoped it didn't give her doubts about staying on the tour with us. The thought of her leaving left me cold.

"Hey," I said, suddenly shy. "Would you have dinner with us tonight? I...have something in mind." Something I hoped she and Channing would like.

"Of course," she said. "Just the three of us?"

"Yeah. Dress all fancy. I'll arrange all the things."

10

ABBIE

I HAD no idea what Landon planned, so it took forever to decide what to wear. I narrowed it down to my little black dress and a cute black skirt and red halter top. I lay them both out on one of the beds and looked back and forth between them about a million times.

"What do you think?" I asked Asher.

He sat on the edge of one of the other beds, watching me watching my clothes as if they would stand up and beg to be put on. I wished they would. That would make the choice easier. Of course I'd go with the outfit that lay there like it wasn't alive and freaking me the fuck out.

"I'm going to assume naked isn't an option?" he asked.

"I don't think so," I said dryly. I mean, stranger things, right? "I just saw Landon disappear into the other room with a bag that looked like it had a suit in it. Not a birthday suit," I added quickly.

Asher snapped his fingers. "Bummer. In that case I say you should go for..." He rubbed his chin and thought.

"The dress. Landon said fancy, didn't he? Dresses like that are universally fancy. Especially when they're lying in a puddle on the floor."

I laughed softly. "Do you think about anything other than sex?"

"Absolutely," he agreed. "Sometimes I think about drumming. Not very often, mind you. I wouldn't want to distract from all the thinking about sex."

Zeke came and sat beside Asher. "Did I hear someone mention sex?" He kissed Asher, then grabbed my hand and pulled me onto his lap. "Are we making plans? Or just getting down to it?" He kissed me lightly, but quickly deepened the kiss. His tongue grazed over my lip, enticing me to forget what I was doing. And maybe my name.

I kissed him back, but then broke it off. "I'm supposed to be getting ready for a date with Landon and Channing."

"Ah, the mysterious date," Zeke said. "He's been

buzzing about it all day, but he won't give anyone any details." He didn't look pleased about that.

"Landon's not going to do anything stupid," Asher said. "He wouldn't risk Channing or Abbie."

"What are we going to do when we get back to Australia?" I asked. "Hole ourselves up in a hotel until the end of time?"

"I don't know," Zeke admitted. "We'll take care of it. Whatever it takes to do that. Even if we have to buy an island and hide out there."

"I'm down for that, if it has Wi-Fi," Asher said.

"It would definitely have Wi-Fi," Zeke said. "And place for a helicopter to land. And a yacht or two. And a bunch of staff to cook and clean for us."

I sighed. "That sounds heavenly. Where do I sign up?"

"Anywhere you like," Zeke said. "As long as you come with us."

"Wait," Asher said. "We need a recording studio too."

"Fuck yeah," Zeke said. "We can fly Candy out to produce our stuff. We're going to need to keep releasing if we're going to afford this island and all the shit on it."

"Blazing Violet and Cameo Orchid can come and record there," Asher said.

I leaned into Zeke and rested my head on his shoulder. If nothing else, it was a nice fantasy. At some point, we'd have to find a way to get back to living in the real world. Would it ever be safe enough to do that though? It had to be. If Zeke said we would deal with it, then we would. One way or another.

"Can we have our own chickens?" I asked. "I've always wanted to have chickens. They're so cute and fresh eggs are so nice."

"If you want chickens, then we're having chickens." Zeke nodded.

"I can see children chasing them around," Asher said. "Little blond-haired kids who look just like me."

"That would be sweet," Zeke said, his voice low. "But I'd like at least one to look like me." He looked at me with dark eyes.

What could I say to that? I wasn't ready to think about next week, much less children. One for each guy was a lot of children. Would they all even want that? That was a question for another day. Maybe another year.

"I don't think it's very nice to encourage children to chase chickens," I said. "Although, from what I know about chickens, they're more likely to chase children. Especially the roosters."

"Would we need a rooster?" Asher asked. "I think we have enough cocks as it is." He chuckled.

I laughed too. "We'll put a rooster on the maybe pile." Along with all of those children.

"And if the rooster chases any children, we'll put it on the barbecue," Zeke said, a broad grin on his face.

"Are you going to kill it?" Asher asked. "Or take a hit out on it? Maybe Tully could use his ninja skills to do it."

"What am I using my ninja skills on?" Tully sat down on the bed beside my two outfits, careful not to sit on them.

He shook his head after Asher explained. "I don't think I could kill an innocent animal."

Asher opened his mouth, but closed it again.

I guessed he was going to say Tully would kill a rooster if it tried to kill him first, but thought better of it.

Judging by the expression on Tully's face, he saw the same thing. His eyes took on a haunted look until he shook his head and managed to smile.

"I'm sure you can find someone to do the deed," Tully said lightly.

"Maybe we should just not get a rooster," I said.

"While you're all here, I could use all your input on what outfit to wear tonight."

"We've already ruled out her going naked," Asher said helpfully.

"Shame." Tully clicked his tongue. "You could wear one of my T-shirts. You'd look cute like that."

"Yes I would," I said. "But I don't think that's what Landon had in mind when he said fancy." Or maybe he did and I had it all wrong. I didn't think so though.

"My T-shirts are very fancy." Tully sniffed and pretended to look offended. "You could put a belt around your waist and a pair of heels."

"Why does that sound so fucking hot?" Asher asked.

"It does, doesn't it?" Zeke asked.

"I don't have a belt." I shrugged. I had to agree, the outfit would look adorable.

"You could use the cord I use to charge my phone," Asher offered. "What could be hotter than a USB cord wrapped around you?"

"Just about everything?" I said tentatively. I made a face at him and laughed. "I'm not going to wear a cable around myself, but thank you for the offer."

"You're welcome," Asher said. "What about shoelaces?"

"What about I wear one of these outfits?" I gestured towards them. "Or I could go and buy something new, but that could take hours." I glanced at my watch. My shopping trips never took that long, but the implied threat that they would have to follow me around while I looked through clothes and tried things on, might hurry the guys up in making up their minds.

"I vote for the black dress," Zeke said quickly.

"Me too," Tully said.

Mission accomplished. I bit back a smile.

"Thank you," I said graciously. I hopped off Zeke's lap and folded up the skirt and halter top. I placed them back in my suitcase and closed the lid. "It really would be nice to go for a shopping trip one day."

"Take Penn." Asher jerked his head in his direction. "He loves shopping for clothes."

Penn, who was sitting on the couch watching cartoons on TV, looked over and nodded. "For once in his life, Asher isn't being sarcastic. I actually do like shopping for clothes."

"We knew there was something wrong with him," Asher said jokingly.

"You could do with a few new outfits," Penn said, looking him up and down critically. "Do you own anything that doesn't have a hole in it somewhere?"

"Of course I fucking do," Asher said in protest. "At least a couple of things."

"This whole conversation is ironic, since we all have clothes with holes in them," Tully said. "We wouldn't look much like rock stars if we were in three-piece suits or brand-new jeans. The kind that look new."

"No, then we would be crooners or pop stars," Asher agreed. "And we're neither of those. Although, we would look sharp in three-piece suits."

"No," Zeke said simply.

"No?" Asher asked.

"No, we're not wearing suits on stage," Zeke said for clarification. "At least, I'm not. You guys can please yourselves I guess." He shrugged. "It's too fucking hot out there for that. We get drenched enough as it is."

"In a word, no fucking way," Penn said.

"That's three words," Tully pointed out.

"Whatever." Penn changed the channel. "Well shit."

"What is it?" I glanced up to see him watching the news. That couldn't be good.

"To the surprise of absolutely no one, Sydney

police have ruled the death of Calista Rossi not an accident," Penn said. "According to forensic evidence, she was dead before she was munched on by sharks. Who knew?"

"Right." I sank down on the bed beside my dress.

"Don't stress. Apparently they found a bunch of blood at Pete's place. They're testing it to see if it matches hers. How much do you want to bet it will?"

"Nothing," I said. "I didn't like her, but I don't want to bet on who or what killed her either." I massaged my forehead with my fingertips.

"Hey." Tully shifted over closer to me and put his arm around me. "At least they know it wasn't you. Her family would want answers, wouldn't they?"

"I guess so," I said. "I mean, I would if I was them." I hadn't met them. If she was anything like them, I wouldn't want to.

Still, they deserved answers. It wouldn't be fair to go around thinking an innocent shark did something they didn't. Poor sharks got enough bad publicity as it was. Even more than I did. They were just big fish who wanted to live their lives. Could they help it if sometimes people got in the way? My philosophy was that if they stayed out of my bath, I would stay out of theirs. So far, that worked pretty well.

"Someone got arrested for throwing a bottle at paparazzi before the concert the other night," Penn continued. "Apparently they got off with a warning. And a ban from attending concerts at the stadium for the next decade." He changed the channel back to cartoons.

"On one hand, that sucks," Asher said. "On the other hand, I don't have any sympathy for people that throw things like that. I'm so conflicted." He scratched the side of his head.

"Actions have consequences," Tully said. "I'm not conflicted."

"Me either," Zeke said. "It's lucky they didn't throw a bottle at us, or I would be facing some hefty consequences right now." He smiled but looked unapologetic.

"They wouldn't have hit us anyway," I pointed out. "We were too far away."

"Then they are the lucky ones," he said. "Because I'm not letting that happen again to any one of us. I'm still pissed off it happened to you."

I touched my cheek lightly. There was a faint scar there from where the can hit me and broke the skin. Asshole could have thrown an empty one. It would have done less damage.

"Me too," I said. Sometimes I dreamt I was on

stage, dodging flying objects. Sometimes they were cans, other times heads. The heads were definitely worse. Each of them had a face: Jonah, Poppy, even Pete. My stomach turned just thinking about it.

I lowered my hand. "I should get ready for this date." I hoped I didn't bring the mood down.

I didn't want to ruin whatever Landon had planned for us.

11

ABBIE

"YOU LOOK BEAUTIFUL," Landon said at the same time as I said, "This is incredible."

We both laughed.

Channing, who was standing over by the table, grinned. "I think everyone likes what they see."

"I certainly do," I agreed, my eyes on both guys.

They each wore a suit, button down shirt and no tie. Landon's suit was blue and his shirt bright yellow, while Channing's was black, over a crisp white shirt. That was their personalities, right there. Landon was flamboyant, Channing understated.

I dragged my eyes off them to admire the room.

Located on the other side of the corridor from our hotel rooms, someone had pushed the furniture off to one side and brought in a dining table and three chairs. Every surface was covered with candles, each a dancing flame flickering in the warm breeze that came through the open doors that led to a balcony.

Another section of the room was left empty of everything except a bunch of rose petals scattered over the hardwood.

"That's the dance floor," Landon explained. "In case we feel like dancing. There's also a really big hot tub. It's big enough for eight, so it should fit three just fine."

"You thought of everything," I said. This was by far the most romantic date I have ever had. Even more than the one with Tully in Perth. Although, the race was closer than the one between Penn and Channing.

Landon poured three glasses of champagne and handed me one.

"He always does," Channing said. "He's the undisputed master of romantic dates." He shot his boyfriend a proud, loving look.

Landon sipped his drink and shrugged, but he seemed to enjoy the praise. "I like to spoil the people I care about. We don't get many nights off, so we should enjoy it."

"It's beautiful," I assured him. "Did you light every candle yourselves?"

Landon glanced at Channing. "I'd love to say we did, but I'd be bullshitting. We had some help from the hotel staff. Otherwise we'd be lighting them for days."

"Hashtag fact," Channing said. "Thank fuck blowing them out is going to be easier. I tried to talk Landon out of having so many, but he insisted." He smiled indulgently.

"Go hard or go home," Landon said with a shrug. "Do you wanna sit?" He put down his drink and pulled out a chair.

"Thank you, kind sir," I said graciously, and sat. How different that would be if I was talking to Penn. For one thing, I wouldn't have put 'kind' in front of 'sir.' 'Harder,' maybe, but not, 'kind.'

Landon even pulled a chair out for Channing, who raised an eyebrow at him but sat. Could they be more stinking cute together?

The funny thing was, I never felt like the third wheel with them. Or with Zeke and Asher. I had a different kind of relationship with each of them and their relationships with each other were different again. No one was competition for anyone else. We all just enjoyed each other's company.

"Food won't be long," Landon said. "I can't take credit for any of that either. Except organising the menu with the kitchen. I hope you like what I chose."

"As long as it's not barbecued rooster, I'm sure I will," I said.

When they both gave me a funny look, I explained the conversation I had with the rest of the guys. I also briefly mentioned the bit about Calista and the person who threw the bottle. I didn't want to dwell on either of those things.

Evidently, neither did the guys because they quickly changed the topic to how good the champagne was.

A knock on the door announced the arrival of the first course. A a member of staff dressed in the hotel uniform wheeled in a trolley. On top were plates with a variety of small finger foods. Tiny quiches, tiny pastries, toothpicks with fruit and cheese. Everything was identical in portions and shapes. That kind of detail must have taken hours. It almost looked too good to eat, but at the same time, I was hungry.

I picked up a mini quiche Lorraine and bit into it. The crumbly, buttery pastry was cooked to perfection, the egg was light and fluffy.

"Mmmm, this is so good." I finished in two bites and reached for a pastry.

"One of the best parts about travelling the world is getting to taste food you didn't make yourself," Landon said.

"At least you can cook," Channing said. To me he added, "He's trying to teach me, but I'm not very good."

"Yes, you are," Landon said around a mouthful of fruit. "Scrambled eggs are tricky."

"They really are," I agreed. "It's easy to overcook them." I did it myself plenty of times. My mother had a knack for them, which I hadn't inherited or learned.

"See?" Landon said to Channing. "It's just a matter of practice. You'll get there, love."

"I'm better at making cakes," Channing said. "Unfortunately, Landon won't let me eat cake for breakfast, lunch and dinner." He grimaced playfully. He slid the fruit sideways off a toothpick and dropped it onto his plate.

"You'd get tired of cake after a while," I said. "Even if it was really good cake."

"That's what I keep telling him," Landon said. "Everything in moderation."

"Even champagne." I wasn't used to drinking the

decent stuff, just the cheap drop from the local bottleshop. The one Landon chose tonight was delicious.

"Even champagne," Landon agreed.

The first course was replaced by the second. Not rooster cooked on a barbecue. Not even chicken. Instead, it was a fancy version of macaroni and cheese. It was absolutely delicious.

"If I eat much more than this, you're going to need to roll me out the door." I patted my stomach.

"Or we can work it off first." Landon winked.

"I should have guessed you'd suggest that," I said teasingly. "Lots of dancing then?"

Both guys laughed at that.

"Lots and lots of dancing," Channing agreed. "Speaking of dancing, should we work up an appetite for dessert?" He looked sideways at us, clearly not proposing we dance vertically. Or, not for very long anyway.

"Yes, we should." Landon jumped up and grabbed his phone from the table. He pressed the screen a couple of times before music started to play. "I was hoping for speakers in the ceiling, but the hotel couldn't get them installed in time. So this will have to do."

He set the phone back down and held out his hand for me to stand.

I took it and we all moved to the dance floor. Landon faced me, and Channing stood behind. They both stepped in close so their bodies were pressed full length against mine.

Channing placed his hands on my hips, just above Landon's. Together, we started to sway, me the meat in a hot-rock-gods-in-suits sandwich.

Fuck yes.

In a matter of moments, their erections were pressed against me. Just in time for me to be as wet as fuck. There goes another perfectly good pair of panties, I sighed to myself.

Honestly, my laundry bill for panties alone must be almost as big as the cost of the entire tour. If the label wanted me to pay, I was going to pass it on to the guys. Most of it was their fault anyway. Knowing them, they'd happily pay it.

Men.

"Hot tub, balcony, bed, or wait until after dessert?" Landon asked.

"Yes," Channing said. His chest rumbled against my back.

Landon snorted. "Okay, all of the above, but which first?"

"Why choose?" Channing asked. "Can we take the bed and hot tub out to the balcony and fuck while eating desert?"

"I admire your ambition," Landon said. "But the hot tub weighs about a million kilos and is tiled into the bathroom."

I giggled at how silly this conversation was. It was adorable how comfortable they were with each other. I liked how they fitted me into their lives without a second thought. At least no second thoughts I saw. They both seemed to be as all in as I and the other guys were.

"There's always—" I started to say. I was interrupted by the arrival of the dessert trolley. "Fucking hell." We all sprang apart.

"Long time no see," Hunter Brantley said. He was dressed in a dark blue suit. His twin brother Parker was right behind him, dressed in dark grey. "I offered to bring the dessert up and they were happy to let me help." He smiled.

"Actually, we swiped the dessert trolley," Parker said. "We thought we'd surprise you."

"It looks like we did." Hunter grinned.

"What the fuck do you want?" Channing growled. He'd turned so Landon and I were behind him.

"Honestly," Hunter said slowly, "I'd love some of

the desert on this tray." He picked up a cloche and peeked at the plate underneath. "Looks good, doesn't it?" He poked a finger into the middle of the chocolate mousse, then stuck it in his mouth.

"Mmmm, that's really good. Park, you should try some."

"I'm trying to watch my figure," Parker said. He placed his hands on his hips and wiggled.

"What do you really want?" I asked coldly. Apart from ruining our evening and our dessert. There was no way I'd touch it after Hunter had. Truthfully, there's no way I'd touch it knowing either of them were anywhere near it. Fuck knows what they might have slipped into it. Probably something nasty, dangerous and illegal.

"Oh, hi Abbie." Parker gave me a little finger wave. "I didn't see you there hiding behind these two clowns. Funny, I would have thought they would hide behind you. How's Penn, by the way? No hard feelings there, I hope? We were just doing what we were told. Except the part about telling you where he was. That was kind of a peace offering, in case our dear brother decided to go to Reuben."

"Penn is fine, no thanks to you," I said. "I suggest you stay away from him unless you want your nuts ripped off and roasted over a campfire."

Hey, that was creative. Go me.

"Feisty, aren't you?" Hunter asked. He picked up a bowl of chocolate mousse and a spoon and started to eat. Not the one he'd struck his finger into. Fucking brat. "If you ever get tired of those losers, you should look Parker and I up. We'll show you how real men fuck."

"Don't you have a girlfriend?" I asked. "Real men don't cheat."

"No, but Lila wouldn't mind if you joined us," Hunter said without batting an eyelash.

"I'd rather fuck a potato," I said.

"As evidenced by your presence in the room with these two." Parker grinned.

Channing growled. Landon grabbed his arm to stop him from lunging at the evil twins.

"They're not worth it," Landon said. "Sooner or later, they are going to piss off the wrong people and end up in a shallow grave. I for one won't shed a fucking tear."

"Me either," I said.

Parker clicked his tongue. "That's not very nice."

"You're not very nice," I retorted. "Now tell us what you want and then get the fuck out of here. Before we call security."

"There's no need to be like that." Hunter put

down the half-eaten chocolate mousse and stuck his spoon into the third bowl, which hadn't been touched until now.

What a prick.

"We just came to say hello," Hunter added. "And let you know we're still hanging around. Reuben wanted us to remind you that we exist and he exists and all that shit." He shrugged.

"We've been trying to forget, but we haven't managed it," I said. "Maybe next time send us a text message. Or better yet, go back to Sydney and tell Reuben to fuck off."

Parker winced. "Personally, I wouldn't do that. And I promise you, you don't want us to do that either. Reuben gets pissy when people tell him to fuck off."

"Is there anything he doesn't get pissy about?" I asked.

The evil twins exchanged a glance.

"Not really," Hunter admitted. "Anyway, we've delivered our message. We'll be on our way. Have a great rest of your night." He and Parker ducked out the door.

We all sagged against each other.

"We should tell Zeke," I said softly.

"Before or after we blow out all these candles?" Channing asked.

I sighed. We didn't need to talk about it to know we were in agreement not to stay here after that visit.

What I wanted to do now was hide under the blankets with as many of my guys around me as possible.

12

ABBIE

"THOSE LITTLE FUCKERS!" Zeke growled. He started towards the door but stopped a couple of metres from it.

"They'll be long gone by now. I should have been there. I would have kicked their asses into the next millennia. Or the one after that." His face was red with fury.

Asher and I moved to comfort him and bumped into each other. He put out a hand to steady me, and we both half laughed.

"Sorry." I slipped an arm around Asher and another around Zeke. "I wholeheartedly support your desire to kick their asses. They freaked the fuck out of me when they walked into the room."

"I'll bet they did." Zeke pulled me closer so my head was resting against his shoulder.

Asher did the same on the other side so we were all pressed together, sharing heat and muscle.

"Not to mention the waste of chocolate mousse," Asher groaned.

"That might just be the worst part of all," I said, grimacing against the smooth fabric of Zeke's shirt. It wasn't the worst part, not even close, but whatever it took to lighten the mood.

The twins scared the crap out of me without even trying, without even threatening us or waving guns at us. They'd assaulted me and Penn, I had no idea how far they might go on Reuben's orders. I didn't particularly want to find out. If it was worse than what they'd already done, then it would be pretty fucking horrible.

"I'm sorry," Zeke whispered so only we could hear. "I should have dealt with them somehow. They've been a thorn in my side for so long. If I'd known they were going to haunt us on this tour…"

"What could you do?" Asher asked. "You're not the kind of person who goes around killing indiscriminately. You did what you could to distance yourself from the rest of the family. What's left after that?"

Zeke's shoulder twitched when he shrugged slightly. "Beat the shit out of them until they promise to leave us alone?" He sighed. "Yeah, I know. I wouldn't have done that either. Even if it's a good idea. Maybe I need to rethink my attitude towards gratuitous violence."

"Reuben would love that," Asher said ironically. "Right before he welcomes you back into the family and closes the door behind you. That's the whole reason you walked away, remember?"

"Not the whole reason," Zeke said softly. He pressed the side of his face against Asher's and smiled down at me. "I wanted to know the people I love weren't going to get stuck in the middle of some gangland war. It happened anyway."

"If this is where you say, maybe we should break up to keep us safe, no deal," I said firmly. "We're in this with you until the end. No matter what happens. I'm not walking away from you."

Even as I said that, my heart raced. If he wanted to walk away from me, from us, I couldn't stop him. Not really. When it came down to it, we had only known each other for a few months. Everything was still new and fragile.

But fuck, losing either of them would break my heart.

"Hell no, we're not going anywhere," Asher said. "Whatever you do, no matter how stupid, we'll stand by you. I'll hold one of them down for you while you beat them up if you want. Whatever you need."

Zeke smiled a little broader, but still with restraint. "I'd like to think it won't come to that. But if those little pricks come near either of you again, all bets are off."

I had the feeling if the twins were in front of him right now, they'd both get a one way trip off the balcony. It wasn't high enough to kill them, but it might break a few bones. That would slow them down. Not to mention, it might be fun. For us.

I should probably not enjoy that thought as much as I did. Fuck it, you couldn't go around scaring the shit out of people without them thinking nasty thoughts about you. That was how the universe worked.

"Where's Channing?" Zeke asked after a couple more minutes of fuming.

"He took the dessert cart back down to the restaurant," Landon said. "He wanted to make sure they didn't kill anyone. I was going to go with him, but I thought it was better to bring Abbie back here first."

Zeke hesitated, but then nodded. "As long as he

stays inside the hotel, he should be okay. But if he doesn't come back soon, we'll go looking for him."

Landon nodded, then jumped at a knock on the door. He hurried over to look through the peephole, then opened it to let Channing inside.

"Thank fuck," Landon said. "I was starting to worry." He wrapped his boyfriend in a bear hug.

Channing patted his back. "I'm fine. The kitchen didn't even notice the trolley was missing. All of the staff seem to be accounted for. They said they'd send up some more chocolate mousse for everyone."

"Fuck yeah," Penn said. He and Tully had stayed sitting on the couch, listening while Landon and I told them what the twins did. They looked equally pissed off as each other.

Okay, maybe Penn edged out Tully a little. He would hold his grudge against Hunter and Parker until the end of time, if not longer. Which was totally understandable. What they did to him was grudgeworthy, and then some.

"I love chocolate mousse," the keyboardist added.

"Doesn't everyone?" Tully rose and moved to grab a T-shirt from his suitcase. He tossed it to me. "In case you want to change out of that dress."

I caught it before it hit the floor. "Thanks. I think I'm ready to look a bit less fancy now." After the way the date ended, I might just stick to casual clothes and group activities from now on. Safety in numbers and all that.

"I can't guarantee you'll look less fancy." Tully grinned. "You could make a paper bag look sexy."

"Is it wrong that I'd like to see that some day?" Asher asked.

"I don't know if it's wrong," Zeke said. "But it is a bit weird." He gave Asher a funny look.

"Since I'm a bit weird, then that works out perfectly," Asher said cheerfully. "I'll keep an eye out for a paper bag the right size."

"That sounds like one of those fashion shows where they like to push the envelope," I said. I kicked off my heels and started to change. Since all of them had seen me naked several times before, I didn't even think twice about doing it in front of them.

Neither did Landon and Channing, who started to strip off their suits and put on boxer shorts for sleeping in.

"You might start a new trend," Zeke said. "Paper bag couture."

"Yeah." I snorted. "It's all fun and games until it rains."

"Why does that sound so fucking hot?" Asher groaned.

"You first," I told him. I pulled Tully's T-shirt down into place. It hung almost to my knees. The funny thing was, he probably thought he was getting it back someday. Ha ha, nope, it was mine now. I felt cute in it and it smelled like him. For some reason, that was incredibly comforting. It was like a block of chocolate, a glass of wine and a blanket fort, all rolled into one.

Penn laughed loudly. "Asher wearing a paper bag. That's fucking funny."

Asher flipped him off. "For your information, I'd look adorable." He also started getting ready for bed. "I don't think they make paper bags big enough to fit on me though."

"We could find one," Zeke said. He stripped off his jeans and actually folded them before he put them into suitcase. "Or have one made. What's the point of having money if you can't have people make weird shit for you?"

In spite of his banter, and the smile on his mouth, Zeke's eyes showed he was still worried and annoyed.

I hoped he wasn't planning to do something stupid. Partly because he might get hurt and partly because we would all follow him into it. I didn't think there was a person in the room who wouldn't follow him to the end of the Earth and back. Even if we all ended up in trouble because of it.

Fortunately, no one was naked when a hotel staff member knocked on the door and wheeled in a trolley with seven fresh bowls of chocolate mousse, cups and a pot of fresh coffee.

"Oh my God, that smells so good." I inhaled the heavenly scent, but stayed back until the woman left and Tully firmly locked the door behind her.

"I feel like we're having a sleepover party," Penn said. He had also stripped down to his boxer shorts.

Asher grinned. "It does feel like that, doesn't it? Zeke and I used to sleep over at each other's houses all the time."

"Or tell our parents we were sleeping over and then go somewhere else," Zeke said. He picked up a bowl and spooned some mousse into his mouth. It wasn't until he swallowed, waited and didn't die, that he waved for us to grab some too.

"Yeah, like to the park to get wasted on a bottle of cheap alcohol," Asher said.

"That sounds like fun," Landon said softly. He grabbed a bowl and a cup and went to sit on the end of one of the beds. He wore bright red boxer shorts with a superhero logo all over them.

I grabbed mine and sat beside him. "You didn't

get to do sleepovers?" I asked as gently as I could. "Even in foster care?"

I could understand why he wouldn't want friends over with his mother around. Kid-Landon wouldn't have wanted his friends to see her like that, even if his mother allowed it. That was the kind of thing kids never let other kids forget.

"Not really," he said, his eyes down. "I never really wanted to. It was easier to let the other kids assume I lived with my parents and had a normal life like them."

My heart broke for him. "That must have been rough." I could just imagine the things the other kids would say if they knew what he was going through. He would have been teased and ostracised. It was painfully sad to think he had to pretend just to get by.

The bed dipped as Channing sat on the other side of him. "You have us now and we can have all the sleepovers you want. You'll still have to pretend you hang out with normal people though." He grinned.

Landon snorted softly. "Nah, I gave up on that part of the dream a long time ago." He bumped his shoulder playfully into Channing's.

"Apparently normal is overrated anyway," I said. I dipped my spoon into my chocolate mousse and scooped out a mouthful. "Mmmm, this is the seventh tastiest thing in the room."

"That's very specific," Tully said. He cocked his head at me and slowly licked mousse of his spoon like he was fucking it.

I watched, mesmerised, until he dipped the spoon back into his dessert.

"Yeah," I agreed, blinking to break the spell. "Nothing could be tastier than you six." Their cocks, tongues and the rest of them.

"Then this is the eighth tastiest thing in the room," Landon said. "Because you are definitely delicious." He leaned over and kissed my mouth. He tasted of a divine combination of chocolate and coffee, with a little touch of salt.

If I could bottle that flavour, I would be a billionaire.

"Ninth," Penn said. "Because this mousse is good, but nothing beats coffee."

None of us could disagree with that.

While I ate and drank, I kept half an eye on Zeke. I could almost hear him stewing over his brothers turning up like that. I wanted to tell him not to worry about it, that I wasn't that scared. That was a flat out lie and we all knew it. Seeing them again had me rattled as fuck. That they could so brazenly walk into the room of a hotel in Vienna, without breaking a sweat, without even blinking…

Yeah, I got the message all right. They could and would turn up whenever and wherever they wanted.

That was what scared me most of all.

13

LANDON

WHEN I WAS A KID, I used to think Vienna was some kind of desert. The fancy kind people only got when they were rich. It wasn't until I was in high school I realised it was a place. And now, here I was, standing on a huge stage in Vienna looking out at the crowd.

With a craving for chocolate covered ice cream. Yeah, I have a sweet tooth. Especially when it came to chocolate.

Zeke moved back and forth across the stage with his usual energy. Some nights, he was exhausting to watch. Other nights, I itched to move around up there with him.

I glanced over at Channing and knew he was thinking the same thing. If he could, he'd be dancing around with his saxophone for the entire ninety minutes, until sweat dripped off him, drenching his clothes until they stuck to his body, to the ridges of his muscles, the hard plane of his stomach, the V of his hips.

The downside to him playing saxophone, was that he more or less had to stay put, like me. The two of us and Asher were the backbone of the band, but as the spine we had to stay at the back. That suited me.

Channing, well, he usually tried to fit in a workout before we went on stage. To work off that nervous energy.

"Vienna, you are fucking nuts!" Zeke shouted into the mic. "You're the best, wildest audience all tour! Maybe ever!"

Of course, the crowd loved hearing that. Just like the crowd loved hearing it every concert we'd done so far, even though they probably knew he said that every time. It was all part of the fun of going to a rock concert.

As far as I knew anyway. I'd only ever been to school concerts before I joined Wolf Venom. Even now, the ones I went to were by acts signed with our label. They were more than happy to hand a few tickets around to us. I'd never been to see anyone just for the hell of it.

When did I have the time? If I wasn't touring, I was busy with something else to do with the band. I was always the first to put my hand up for interviews, guest appearances, or playing on other people's albums. If I made myself indispensable, then they would keep me around for longer. Right?

Yeah, I know some people would think it was stupid that I was insecure. I played bass guitar for the biggest, best rock band on the face of the planet. I should have an ego as big as the sun. I tried to act like I did, but there was always that voice in the back of my mind that told me I wasn't good enough and that sooner or later everyone would leave.

Realistically, the band might break up some day. The other guys wouldn't have an excuse to hang out with me anymore. Except Channing. Him I was sure of.

Abbie—confidence in her might take a bit longer. I wanted to be sure of her, one hundred percent, but that same little voice told me I wasn't good enough for her.

Okay, that little voice told me I wasn't good enough for Channing either, but I had to believe him when he told me I was. I *wanted* to believe it.

I watched him put his saxophone to his beautiful mouth and make gorgeous music. Bass was the best instrument ever, of course, but some days I wished I could play saxophone too. Channing tried to teach me, but I didn't have his or Penn's talent for it. I could play both kinds of guitar so there was that.

Even my insecure brain could admit I was good at it.

I grooved as I played, lost in the music, my bass in perfect harmony with Asher's drums. If any of the others made a mistake, no one would notice, at least not as much. If Asher I screwed up, it would throw everyone off. Everything they played and sang was to the rhythm we made.

Asher liked to say that we were the unsung heroes of the band. I agreed with that. When the audience danced and clapped, they were doing it along with us, not Zeke, Tully or Penn. Not even Channing.

Not even Abbie.

I was still furious after those twin pricks ruined our date. The look of fear on her face made me want to hide her away somewhere safe forever. Not in a weird, stalker way, but to protect her.

Channing felt the same way. After chocolate mousse and coffee, he'd told me, in whispers, how angry he was.

"I was ready to take that spoon," he growled, "and shove it down until it came out his ass."

"That's very graphic." I snuggled into his side. "Is your arm that long?"

He snorted with half amusement, half annoyance. "It wouldn't need to be. I'd squash him down like an accordion, until his chin touched his feet. Then I'd do the same thing to the other one."

I chuckled, even though the conversation was slightly disturbing. "I don't know if that's hot or if you've just watched too many cartoons. Maybe you should stop watching TV with Penn."

"You don't think I can do it hmmm?" His fingers slid down my side.

"If anyone could, it would be you," I whispered. "Maybe Zeke. Zeke is pretty fucking strong."

"Yeah, but would Zeke do this?" He flicked his tongue against my neck.

"Not to me," I said. A shiver of desire passed through me. My cock had not forgotten that the twins interrupted at the worst possible time.

All right, even if we weren't interrupted, my cock would still stand up when Channing touched me like that.

"Are you guys still awake?" Abbie whispered.

"Yeah," Channing whispered back. "What's up?"

"Can I sleep next to you? Asher was snoring in my ear."

The sound of the drummer's roars was like a plane engine. I didn't blame her for not wanting to hear that up close.

"Of course you can, honey," I said.

Channing and I shifted over to make room for her.

"We might not sleep for a while," Channing warned.

After a moment, she said, "I wasn't tired anyway."

"The old men went to sleep and left you hanging?" Channing asked teasingly.

For a moment I thought that was what happened. She was only over here as a last resort.

"I wanted to finish what we started," she said. "Without the interruptions this time."

"Sounds good to me," Channing said.

The next thing I knew, he rolled her over until she was lying on her stomach on top of me.

"Um, hello there," I said. For someone with such presence, she weighed almost nothing. Well, not nothing, but she was light, her curves soft under my hands.

"Hey," she said before she kissed my mouth.

I slipped my hands up the back of her thighs and

over her perky ass. I rucked up her shirt and slid my hands across her bare back. Her skin was so smooth under my fingertips. If my calluses bothered her, she didn't show any sign. She might like the way they felt. Channing did, as much as I liked his. Extra texture meant extra sensation.

In the faint light that filtered through the curtains, I saw Channing move around behind her. He hooked his hands through the top of her panties and slid them off her ass and down her legs.

She lifted her feet to help him pull them off before he tossed them aside.

He moved back up and his face disappeared between her legs. All I could see past her perfect, round ass, was the top of his head.

She let out a soft, sighing moan as he started to work her with his mouth. Her breasts brushed my chest, her nipples hardening with the contact. My cock hardened along with them.

She must have felt it because she wriggled against me. Her hand slipped down between us to grip my length. She had absolutely no mercy. She wound her hand up and down me like a corkscrew, firm and fast like she was determined I would come so hard I blew my head off.

I groaned and bucked against her driving fingers.

My eyes were half closed, but they popped open when she slid down my body.

"That's better," Channing whispered. He dove back between her legs, but he'd moved her so her mouth was beside my aching, needy cock.

"Just a little," I agreed as she licked at the bead of precum which wept from my slit, then teased down to my balls and back up again with the tip of her tongue.

I didn't even try to hold back the groan that slipped from my mouth when she drew my cock into hers. She felt so different to Channing. Apart from the fact she didn't have stubble grazing my body. Her mouth was smaller, but softer. Where his was firm and demanding, hers was giving and tight. One wasn't better than the other, they were just different. Awesomely so.

Her breath became a series of ragged pants and sighs before she gasped and shuddered on top of me.

Channing said something to Abbie that I couldn't hear past the blood pounding in my ears.

I figured it out a moment later when she let go of me with her mouth and scooted back up the bed. She rolled us over so I was lying on top of her.

Channing disappeared for a moment, before returning with a tube of lube in his hand.

Hell yeah.

I knelt between Abbie's spread thighs and rubbed my fingers lightly over her saturated pussy. She was so unbelievably wet and warm. Just feeling her like that made me harder than ever.

I positioned my cock outside her entrance and pressed myself slowly into her body. My cock was surrounded by the most incredible, delicious heat, like a velvet pocket. If pockets were between a gorgeous set of thighs.

At the same time, Channing liberally, but meticulously, spread lube around and inside my ass and over his cock. He took the greatest care to make sure I was as wet as Abbie. By the time he was done, I was aching for him, my body begging to be filled.

He tossed the tube aside and gripped my hips with firm, demanding fingers. His cock probed for my ass, hard and as needy as I was. He positioned himself and paused for a heartbeat or two.

When he moved again, he was as relentless as Abbie was with her hand. He pushed himself inside me, only pausing occasionally to let me stretch to take him until he was seated deep.

My whole body was a mess of sensation from front to back. If I even tried to talk right now, it wouldn't be coherent. The only thought I could manage was something about enjoying being so close to two people I cared so much about.

Love, the back of my mind whispered. *You love them both.*

I would unpack that later, at a time when I could think straight.

Slowly, I started to thrust into Abbie.

Channing, who was usually the dominant partner out of the two of us, matched my rhythm instead of insisting I match his. When I slowed, he slowed. When I reached the edge of the precipice and needed more friction, he went faster too.

Fortunately, I didn't have to decide what felt better, me inside her or him inside me, because I couldn't have. They both felt beyond incredible. Filling and being filled at the same time had never felt so...fulfilling.

Even our breathing was in sync, all three of us. Abbie's came in soft little gasps. Channing's was a deeper, heavier grunt and mine, mine was somewhere in the middle. The backbone of the band again.

I worked my hands under her knees and brought her legs up over my shoulders. At the same time, I bent over her more, to let Channing drive in deeper. With every stroke, we were both balls deep now.

"Fuck yeah," Channing grunted.

At least one of us was capable of speech. I may never be able to put a full sentence together again. Good thing I was the bassist, not the lead singer. For so many reasons.

Abbie trembled underneath me and I knew she was close to coming again. That brought me closer still, but I wasn't ready to let go yet. I wanted them both to get off first. Was that gentlemanly or just my need to please people?

Whatever, no one complained. Yet.

Abbie's breath got faster, and she was bucking against me, her clit grazing against my stomach each time I thrust. "Hell yeah," she breathed. "Oh my God, that feels so good."

She groaned and shattered underneath me, bucking harder and panting out her orgasm. Her breath was a series of soft pants out her mouth and nose. The noise alone was almost enough to make me come.

I bit my lip to stop myself, and went on thrusting, while at the same time clamping my muscles around Channing as hard as I could.

"Fucking hell, Lan, that's…" Apparently he couldn't speak much either, because he trailed off and pounded into me with even, forceful strokes. "I'm going to come, love."

"Please," I begged. "Please come inside me." Right now, that was the last thing left on my wish list; for him to feel good, for my body to do that for him.

He muttered something incoherent and came, slamming himself over and over again until it stung, but I wouldn't tell him to stop. Not until he was done.

He cried out, his fingers digging hard into my hips. He drove himself once, twice more, then fell still, gasping and sagging against my back.

I huffed out a gusty sigh and let myself come, the sensation like a rush of heat and fireworks that started in the base of my balls and erupted through them and out the end of my cock. Cum blasted from me, filling Abbie's gorgeous pussy to the brim.

I slumped over her, panting and tired, but satisfied.

I came back to myself as the song ended. Good thing I had a guitar to cover my groin until my erection softened again.

14

ABBIE

"WELL THIS IS NEW," I said uncomfortably.

"It's the label's way of connecting better with fans," Jackson said.

"Yeah, I guess it will do that," I agreed.

The room was like a panel at one of those pop culture conventions. Instead of a table, the guys sat on chairs on the stage, while people who paid good money to see them had tiered seating in the small auditorium. A couple of the tour's support staff wore Wolf Venom T-shirts and carried microphones.

Lucky for me, I got to stand off to the side with Jackson and watch.

Landon and Channing looked as uncomfortable as I felt. Tully sat up in his chair like he was at school. Asher, Zeke and Penn all reclined in their chairs like they were couches. Zeke and Asher looked happy to be there. Penn had his usual scowl on his face.

"This is going to be interesting," I said softly. With any luck, Penn wouldn't offend anyone. Honestly, I doubted he'd give a shit if he did.

The host of the Q and A was a tall, model-gorgeous brunette, with big breasts and a perfect body. She had the kind figure I wished I had. Slender in a sporty kind of way. I could work out for a hundred years and still not look like that.

None of the guys seemed to notice her, but she definitely noticed them. Her eyes followed them around, attentive like a hawk.

She put a microphone to perfectly painted, bright red lips and smiled while looking at them through her lashes.

"Good afternoon." She spoke flawless English with an Austrian accent. "My name is Valentina Wagner. I would love to welcome you to this question and answer session with the fabulous band, Wolf Venom."

"Who is she again?" I whispered.

Jackson shrugged. "Some local entertainment reporter. Apparently she's famous in Austria." He sounded as impressed as the guys, but I'd seen the way he looked at her when we first walked in. Not that I could blame him. If I was into women, I'd drool over her too.

The audience clapped. They were obviously excited, judging by their smiles and the way they all looked ready to leap out of their seats, but they were more reserved than a concert audience. So far.

"Let us first let the boys introduce themselves." Valentina walked over on her stiletto heels and leaned forward to make sure the microphone in Zeke's hand was turned on. Of course in order to do that, she had to bend over so her breasts were right in front of his face.

He raised his eyebrows and moved his head back until she stepped away.

If she noticed his discomfort, she showed no sign. She was either professional, oblivious or both.

One by one, the guys said their names into the microphone and passed it on. Each time, the audience clapped and a couple of people wolf whistled.

"Now we'll open for questions," Valentina said when they were done. "Raise your hand and my friends will bring a microphone to you."

Almost every hand in the place rose.

The first to ask a question was a boy of about eight. He had pale blond hair, bright blue eyes and looked nervous as hell as he spoke into the microphone.

"What is your favourite song that you play?" His question out, he sat down with a plop.

"Do I have to pick a favourite?" Zeke asked, speaking first because the microphone was back in his hand. "Okay, um. 'Rock out with You.'"

He passed the microphone on down the line until it reached Asher. Instead of answering, he looked at the boy and asked, "Which is your favourite?"

The boy, his face bright red, stood up again and said, "I watched on social media when Penn played 'Hallelujah'. That was my favourite." He sat down again.

Penn grinned and leaned over to speak into the microphone. "Good choice. You clearly have great taste."

The audience laughed.

The next question was from a curvaceous blond who couldn't have been more than about nineteen or twenty years old. "I have a question for Zeke."

Asher handed the microphone over.

"Hey, how are you?" Zeke asked. His gaze was on her like she was the only person in the room. He had a way of making people feel like he genuinely cared about the answer. Like in that moment he knew she existed and that she mattered.

"Good," she squeaked.

"You have a question for me?" he asked, his gaze unwavering. That look would make any girl ruin her panties. It was doing it for me.

"Yeah, I do. Will you marry me?" the young woman giggled.

"There's always one," Jackson muttered.

I rolled my eyes. "There always will be." Whatever. Her fantasy couldn't hurt me, or my relationship with Zeke. It made me more uncomfortable than I already was, but that would pass.

Zeke smiled. "That's very flattering, thank you, but I'm spoken for." He handed the microphone back to Asher without a glance at him or me. If the question bothered him, he showed no sign. It seemed likely he got proposals so often they were quickly forgotten.

The woman pouted and sat back down, but the smile never left her face. She got to speak to her idol. It wasn't something she'd soon forget.

The next question was from a man in his mid-thirties. The band had fans of all ages. The youngest person here was around five and the oldest looked to be in their seventies. You're never too young or too old to appreciate good music.

"Do you think you will ever retire from playing?" the man asked.

It was Asher who answered. "A couple of months ago, I would have told you I'll keep playing and touring until I die. But recently I've started to think that maybe there is a life after music. I'm not ready to step away yet, but I see a day in a few years' time that I might."

All of the guys nodded their agreement.

"Thank you." The man nodded back and sat down.

The next to ask was another young woman. She had pin straight black hair and lips that looked unnaturally plump. She wore the tiniest dress I've ever seen. I was almost certain she had no panties on underneath. If she bent over, the whole room would see her ass and pussy. I had a feeling there were six guys on the stage she wanted to have look at her.

"Hello," she purred into the microphone.

"Hey," Asher said back into the one he still held. "You have a question for one of us?"

"Actually, I have a question for Abbie," she said. She looked straight over to where I was standing.

Valentina looked uncertain. Clearly she hadn't

expected this to happen and wasn't sure what to do. Like the professional she was, she rallied quickly. She turned to me and gave me the kind of smile a woman gives to another when they think they are beneath them somehow. As if she was certain she was thousand percent more gorgeous than I was.

She might be right, but she didn't need to be a bitch about it.

"Abbie Hart, darling, would you like to come out here?" she asked smoothly.

Resisting the urge to give a sarcastic smile and tell her to fuck off, I looked up at Jackson. I half hoped he would say no.

"It's up to you." He gave me an encouraging smile but looked questioning at the same time.

By that, I assumed he meant this event wasn't for me, but the publicity for the label wouldn't hurt. If I decided to stay over here, he would support me, I knew that. All of the guys would.

On the other hand, the audience would remember. No doubt it would get blown up later into something ridiculous. The press might suggest I had something to hide or some shit like that.

I smiled sweetly. "Of course I will."

I stepped out onto the stage and caught Landon's

eye. He glanced towards the audience and gave me a secretive grin.

I had to hold back a laugh at his suggestion that we'd even consider fucking in front of them. That was definitely his thing all right.

Predictably, the moment I had that thought, a bolt of heat went right to my core. He knew how to get to me with just a look. Then again, they all did. These days, it didn't take much. At this rate, they'd have to empty the rig truck and make room for spare changes of panties for me.

I considered sitting on one of the guy's laps to answer the question, but thought better of it. Instead, I walked over to take the microphone from Asher. He let his fingers brush over mine a little more than they should, and grinned.

He was as big a brat as Landon.

I looked up into the audience to find the woman and gave her the warmest smile I could. Meanwhile, my palms were sweating and my heart was racing.

Please, please, please, don't say something horrible. It had occurred to me she might have asked me to come out here to tell me to fuck off and leave the guys alone. Nothing much would surprise me these days.

"You're touring with one of the most amazing

bands ever," the woman said. "Six—I think we can agree—hot guys." She smiled down at them.

I had no idea where this was going, but I nodded.

"I am and, yeah, they're okay." I smiled at them and tried not to laugh when they made faces at me.

"How do you deal with that?" the woman asked. "I mean, it's difficult enough for women in the music industry anyway, right? Take today. They're on centre stage and you're off to the side. Shouldn't you be out there with them? A generation of girls is looking up to you and you're being pushed aside. Doesn't it make you angry?"

Okay, I hadn't expected any of that. She made a lot of very good points. Good enough that I had to take a moment to give her a genuine, thoughtful response.

"I'm not gonna lie," I said. "It is hard. A lot of the stuff that's happened to me over the last couple of years would have been different if I was a guy. If a man married a woman for twenty-six hours he probably did it because she wouldn't sleep with him, or because she told him she was pregnant, or whatever. That's the story the press would tell. She'd be the one vilified."

"Exactly," the woman said. "It's a double standard." She looked genuinely pissed off.

Shit, I felt terrible for judging her based on what she was wearing. Was I any better than the double standard we were railing against? I made a mental note to be less judgy from now on.

"It is, but I was standing on the sidelines because Wolf Venom are headlining this tour. When I'm headlining, if anyone tries to tell me I can't stand in the middle of the stage during a Q and A, I will kick their ass." I grinned.

The audience laughed and almost every woman there cheered and clapped.

"Thank you," the woman handed the microphone back to the support guy and sat.

I gave her a smile and was about to hand the microphone back to Asher when the guy with the next question spoke.

"You claim to know audiences are coming out to see Wolf Venom," he said, his tone pure acid. "Why are you touring with them when no one wants to see a washed up slut?"

Yeah, I should have guessed shit like that was coming. The audience muttered, some angry, some in agreement. The guys looked like they were ready to bound out of their seats and rip the guy's head off.

I held up a hand to let them know I could deal with this. I hoped.

"Excuse me for a moment, I have to ask my manager something," I said.

Still speaking into the microphone, I said to Jackson, "How many countries is 'Inside Out' currently number one on their music charts?"

"At least forty-two," Jackson shouted. He smiled with unbridled satisfaction.

"At least forty-two," I repeated into the microphone. "Nice. I think that answers the question." I handed the microphone back to Asher and walked off the stage to a deafening roar of applause.

15

ABBIE

I slipped out a side door of the auditorium, to a small waiting room close enough to hear but not see. Or be seen.

I flopped down on a couch in the corner to gather my breath and my thoughts.

Footsteps in the corridor outside made me startle, but it was only Jackson who appeared in the doorway. He walked over and sat down heavily beside me.

"According to the saying, there's one in every crowd." He leaned back and crossed his legs so his ankle rested on his knee and one arm lay across on the back of the couch behind me.

"In my experience, more than one," I said dryly. "They're usually not given a platform to stir up shit."

He looked over at me. "Next time I'll have the staff vet the questions before they're asked. That should head off the problem before it becomes one. For what it's worth, most of the audience was behind you."

Yeah, most. Not all.

"I shouldn't let it get to me." I sighed heavily. "I know that, but I've asked myself the same question… I don't know how many times. Why me? Why this tour?"

"Why *not* you? Why *not* this tour?" he countered. "Because Levi thought it would be a good fit. I happen to agree with him." He was the soul of calm and patience right now.

I leaned against the back of the couch, my face raised towards the ceiling, and closed my eyes. "I'm sorry. You have better things to do than nurse singers with fragile egos."

"Nursing rock stars with fragile egos is at the top of my job description," he said. "Just above dealing with drunk ones and ones who behave like dick-heads, and being a spoilsport. Trust me, you have nothing on some of them. Most of them, if I'm honest. Some days it's Asher's smart mouth, or Penn's grumpy ass. Other days it's trying to stop Violet and Blaise from screaming at each other and throwing things. One of these days they're either going to fuck or kill each other. Hopefully not the latter. I wish they'd get on with it. I don't know how the rest of the band puts up with them."

"Sounds like you need danger pay," I said sympathetically. "Especially if people start throwing things. At least the guys only throw food at each other. And insults." That I've seen.

Jackson snorted. "Yeah, there's that. Although Asher once dumped a full pitcher of beer on Penn's head. You can imagine how well that went down."

"Cold and dripping?" I guessed.

He chuckled. "Something like that. Knowing Penn, he deserved it, but what a waste of perfectly good beer."

I'd have to remember to ask them what led to that. I pictured Penn's expression now as he sat drenched in sticky beer and smiled.

"What did Penn do?" I asked. "He would have wanted to get Asher back for doing that?"

"He chased Asher around the room and hugged him until they were both wet, and stank." Jackson smiled softly at the memory.

I grinned. "That sounds hilarious. I would have liked to see that."

"Do me a favour?" he asked. "Please don't ask

them to recreate that moment. Levi wasn't happy to get the cleanup bill from the establishment." He rolled his eyes playfully.

"If they do, I'll ask them to do it outside, and maybe use water instead of beer," I said helpfully. It wouldn't be quite as funny, but seeing them with their clothes stuck to them would be worth it.

"Thanks," he said. "I think."

"I'm sure they've gotten up to all sorts of things over the years," I said, hoping to prompt him into spilling some juicy stories.

"Definitely." He nodded. "Most of them you'll have to ask them about, since I can't tell you. But I can tell you this." He locked his eyes on mine. "They've never been as happy as they are now. Even when they first signed with the label and started to get big. They were ecstatic but…" He frowned as he searched for the right words. "I think they were scared it wouldn't last, or that it was a dream. Whenever a song did well, there was pressure for the next one to do even better. Same with every tour. They handled it pretty well, but they were all insecure. Since they met you, they've, I don't know, become comfortable in their own skin? They don't, 'fake it till they make it,' any more. They've made it and they're enjoying it. Does that make sense?"

"Yeah," I said softly, "it does." I hadn't realised I had that impact on them. I cleared my throat before I got too emotional and cried.

"I can relate to trying to outdo myself," I said, changing the subject before I lost it. "I'm more competitive with myself than with anyone else. I hated the idea of letting anyone down, but I hate letting myself down more. I guess that's why questions like that get to me. I feel like I haven't done enough to prove myself." And if I hadn't, then what the fuck more could I do?

He placed an arm lightly around my shoulders and gave me a gentle squeeze. He watched me while he did it, clearly aware of overstepping any boundaries.

"What would it take to feel like it's enough?" he asked. "Number one in over forty countries? A sell-out world tour or three? Or four? Several Grammy awards? A dozen ARIA awards? A guest appearance with the Wiggles?"

I couldn't contain laugh at the last one. "All of the above? Especially the Wiggles. Who wouldn't want to work with them? When I was younger, I wanted to *be* one of them."

"Just between you and me, so did I," he admitted. "That dinosaur looks like a lot less work than most rock stars."

I laughed, but it faded to a faint smile as I thought about his question. I wanted to give him, and myself, an answer.

"I don't know what it would take," I said finally. "Maybe I'm always going to feel like I'm not good enough. Is that necessarily a bad thing though? It means I have to keep working to get better and better, instead of getting stale and complacent."

"I can't imagine you being either of those things," he said softly. "Especially not stale."

He looked at me with an unreadable expression before he drew his arm away. "I think you and the guys will keep pushing the boundaries until there are no more boundaries to push. Then you'll find some new ones and push those. Isn't that what living is all about? Challenging yourself to do things you never thought you could do?"

"I'd like to think some of it is about enjoying the things you know you can do," I said. "Without having to prove yourself again and again."

He shifted on the lumpy couch. "I sound like an old man, but one thing I've learned is that you can't please everyone. We're not tacos. Or cheese."

"You're not an old man." I twisted around sideways and sat with my knees on the couch. "And even cheese can't please everyone. Some people can't eat dairy."

He spread his hands. "That's exactly my point. Not even something as amazing as cheese can make everyone happy. What hope do people have? All we can do is be the best version of ourselves we can be and hope to survive the day without getting beer dumped on our heads."

"They would never do that to you, would they?" I bit back a laugh. I could certainly see them thinking about it, especially Asher, but dumping beer on your manager sounded like a really bad career move to me. Not as bad as Jackson doing it to them and getting fired, but bad enough.

Jackson raised an eyebrow. "I wouldn't put it past them. They like having fun, especially on tour, in the rare moments they get bored."

"Rare moments indeed," I said dryly.

The audience in the auditorium laughed and I smiled. "Sounds like everyone is having fun in there."

He looked down the bridge of his nose at me. "Do you want to go back?"

"No," I said. "This is their moment. You can go back if you want to."

"And leave you alone with the evil twins wandering around?" He grimaced. "Even if the whole band wouldn't be pissed at me, I wouldn't do it. Those two are trouble."

"That's putting it mildly," I said. Just thinking about them made my heart race and my palms sweat. Honestly, I was relieved Jackson was okay about staying with me, otherwise I would have wandered back into the auditorium after I caught my breath. Now I thought about it, coming here alone was kinda silly. Thank goodness Jackson had the sense to follow me.

"I have security watching for them everywhere we go," he said. "Although, from past experience, they are slippery and good at sidestepping security. I guess that's why their family gets away with so much shit. They know how."

"We've gotten away with a bit of it ourselves," I pointed out. "With their help, sometimes."

"That's unfortunately true," Jackson agreed. "I would prefer not to have to deal with…" His gaze flicked towards the door. "Things like that."

Given he was referring to disembodied heads and dead bodies, I could do nothing but agree with him. No one wanted to deal with shit like that. Except, presumably, whoever cut those heads off. Pete, according to the police. I still had my doubts about that. He could be a dickhead, but a killer?

"Yeah. We're lucky you're so chill about…actually, everything." Without thinking, I asked, "You don't think it's weird that I have a relationship with all of the guys?"

He seemed mildly surprised at the question. "Does it matter what I think?" he asked. "If I tell you it's weird, is that going to change anything?"

"No," I admitted. "So—do you?" I was genuinely curious now.

"Like I said, the guys have never been happier. You seem happy, apart from assholes asking stupid questions. What more is there to think about? Love is love and all that." He crossed his legs and cupped his hands around his knee. "If you feel like you need my blessing, you have it. But I don't think you need it."

"Maybe not," I said slowly. "But I feel better knowing you don't feel uncomfortable with the situation. I mean, you do get to hang around with us a lot and things could easily get awkward."

"If it wasn't for those NDAs, I'd tell you a whole bunch of times things got awkward." He made a face. "After a while, you learn to roll with it. Trust me when I say there's pretty much nothing I haven't seen. Or done, for that matter. It might surprise you to learn I've been around the block a time or two myself. I was a full-time touring musician for years before I gave it up and became a manager."

"Oh, I didn't know that," I said. "What instrument did you play? Wait, let me guess. Bass guitar?"

"Yep. Always destined to be in the background." He shrugged.

"The backbone of the band," I said firmly. He was the kind of guy who supported other people without needing a mountain of accolades himself. I could easily imagine him grooving on stage, bass in his hands, looking cool.

"That too," he agreed. "Don't worry, I'm not so insecure that I don't appreciate the role of the bass player. I was never meant to be out the front in the spotlight. It was never what I wanted. All I wanted to do was play and entertain people. When it became apparent the band was never going to be big, we broke up and I concentrated on helping other bands to entertain people." Wistfully, he added, "It's almost as satisfying."

My heart went out to him. Someone had to manage all of our craziness, but it must have been hard to step aside from something he loved to make room for other musicians.

"Do you still play?" I tucked my knees up under me. The couch was so hard it was difficult to stay comfortable for long. I tried not to think about what might have happened on its surface.

"When I can," he said. "If Levi and I are in the same town and have time." He caught the look of surprise on my face and smiled. "You didn't know Levi was in a band too?"

"I knew he was, but I didn't know you were in the same one," I said. "He played lead guitar, right?"

"Guilty," Jackson said. "And sax. Not at the same time. He always had to be the boss and the centre of attention back then, just like now." While other people might have been resentful of that, Jackson spoke fondly.

Unlike Asher, I didn't think Jackson and Levi were sleeping together, but I bet they had some good times performing together.

That gave me an idea. I just had to figure out how to pull it off.

16

LANDON

"WHERE DO people get off being fuckheads?" I sipped good German beer out of a huge stein. A couple of these and I'd be shitfaced. Right now, I was in the mood for it. Most of the Q and A went smoothly, but I couldn't get that asshole and his nasty question out of my head.

"Some people can't help themselves," Abbie said darkly. She handled it beautifully, but she was still as pissed off as the rest of us, I could tell. The guy had pinpointed her insecurities and attacked her with them. No one would blame her if she wanted to scratch his eyes out.

Hell, I wanted to scratch his eyes out.

"Some people should try harder," Penn said with a grunt.

That was ironic coming from him, but for a change, no one pointed it out.

"Want us to track him down and beat him up?" Asher offered.

I couldn't tell if he was joking or not. "I'd be down for that," I said, in case he wasn't.

"Don't give him the satisfaction," Abbie said reluctantly. "People like that want to feel good about themselves so they do it by trying to drag other people down."

"Is that all that's bothering you?" Tully asked her.

"Is it that obvious?" She gave him a wry smile.

He must be more astute than me, because I hadn't picked up on it until he mentioned it. Now he had, I squinted at her. Yeah, something else was definitely up. And the beer was going right to my head. If I wasn't half buzzed, I would have seen it sooner.

She took a moment to continue. "I feel like shit for assuming the woman who wanted to address sexism in the music industry was going to come on to one of you guys," she admitted. "Or all of you. I looked at what she was wearing, and figured…"

I squinted. How could anyone as beautiful as Abbie think for a moment we'd even notice another woman? Okay, I remembered her, and her tiny dress, but she hadn't even crossed my mind. Not like that.

"That other girl had just proposed to Zeke," Asher pointed out with a grin. He poked his boyfriend playfully in the chest. "When's the wedding?"

Zeke groaned. "To her? Never."

"Yeah, she's way too good for you," Penn teased.

Zeke flipped him off.

"Thanks," Abbie said sarcastically. "Nice of you to suggest he's lowered his standards all the way down to me. And Asher."

"You're too good for him too," Penn said unapologetically. "Asher is about right. They're both dickheads." He ducked when Asher scooped up a handful of peanuts from the bowl in the middle of the table and threw them at him.

"Don't get us kicked out," Channing warned.

"I can see the headline now," I said, a silly grin on my face. "Wolf Venom gets kicked out of Frankfurt beer hall for throwing snacks."

"Update at ten," Asher added.

We all laughed.

"It's all fun and games until someone slips on a peanut," Tully said.

Asher frowned. "I'm pretty sure there's a joke or a pun in there somewhere."

"Someone hurt themselves falling over your nuts?" Zeke suggested.

Asher pointed a finger gun at him. "There you go. That works. It's even plausible, given how big they are."

"It's more accurate to say you are a big nut than you *have* big nuts," Penn said.

Asher shrugged. "Any more than a mouthful would be a waste."

"Fact." I nodded. Although, if I died choking on Channing's balls, there were worse ways to go.

Channing grunted something incoherent.

I leaned against his side and put a hand on his arm. "Are you okay? You seem distracted tonight." It must be contagious.

He twitched and for a moment I thought he was going to pull away from me. "Yeah I'm just..." He let out a huffing breath from his nose. "Can we go somewhere? Just for a couple of minutes."

I started to make a comment about him wanting to take me away for a quickie, but then I saw the serious expression on his face.

"There's a spare table on the other side of the hall." I nodded towards it. "We should be able to talk there."

"Okay. Let's go." He pulled away from me and stood.

I gestured to Zeke that we wouldn't be long and followed Channing.

My heart sat in my throat. The beer lay heavy in my stomach. I couldn't say it wasn't like Channing to be serious all of a sudden, because it was. Every time, it made me anxious as fuck. I always assumed the worst. Like, this time he would break up with me or something.

I slipped into the bench beside him and placed my stein on the table in front of me. Depending on what he said, I might need to drink the rest of it quickly.

"Is everything okay?" I asked. "Did I... Do something wrong?"

Should I apologise for it now or wait until he told me what it was? Right now, I had no idea. Maybe I snored too much. Had he decided he didn't want to bring Abbie into our relationship? Had he decided to quit the band and go home? Had he...

Or I could listen and find out what he had to say.

"No, you didn't do anything," he said quickly. "I just feel like..." He looked down at the table.

Okay, here it came. Was I about to get my heart broken?

"Feel like what?" I asked gently.

"Like..." He hesitated again.

My heart beat so hard it was painful.

"Like I hardly get to see you lately," he said quickly. "I know we spend all day every day together, but I haven't had you to myself. Not with all the other guys around."

"And Abbie?" Was that what this was really about? Spending time with her?

"No. Yes. No." He scrunched up his face. Even troubled, he was absolutely adorable. How did I get so fucking lucky?

"Some of the above?" I suggested. Yes and no covered pretty much everything, without actually covering anything. He was making me more and more confused.

"You might need to help me out here," I said. "Is it yes or no?"

"Both." He sighed in frustration. "I see you with her and how happy you are. I wonder if..."

"I'm starting to think I should tickle it out of you," I said only half joking.

He managed a faint smile. "I'm just wondering if you still want to be with me." He said in a rush. "Sometimes I don't think I'm good enough for you, and if she makes you happy..."

My breath came out in a rush of relief. "Is that

what this is about? You think she makes me happier than you do? That I'm gonna leave you for her?"

My relief might be premature. Just because he wasn't mad at me didn't mean we weren't headed for heartache. I almost held my breath until he spat out what he wanted to say.

Since passing out wouldn't be good for the conversation, I forced myself to breathe.

He looked down into his half drunk beer. "I'm not always the easiest person to get along with." He almost looked like he might cry.

"You're my person, and I love you," I said firmly. "I'm not always the easiest person either. None of us are. We're high strung rock stars. But I'm as sure as ever that we can all make each other happy. If that's still what you want?"

"It is," he said quickly. "I just wanted to make sure we were all reading from the same song sheet."

I covered my hand with his. "We are. Nothing will ever change that. You, me, Abbie, the rest of us, we'll make it work as long as that's what everyone wants. You and I, though, we are rock solid. Harder than my cock when I think about you."

"That's pretty hard," he agreed. He gave me a suggestive, lopsided smile that made my heart flip and my blood run hotter. Could he be any more stinking adorable?

I grinned. "Very hard." I took a moment to take a sip of beer. "Did something happen to provoke this? I've noticed you've been a bit moody since—" I thought for a moment. "Since Vienna? I figured you'd tell me when you're ready."

Which I supposed he had.

"It's been stewing for a while," he admitted. "Since before the tour, I guess. You're so, I don't know... you. You deserve better than someone like me."

"I don't know," I said slowly. "I've never met anyone better than you." Abbie being equally good as him, of course. They were the best two people I knew. The rest of the band weren't too far behind.

"See what I mean?" he asked. "You're beyond sweet." He pressed his forehead to mine. "How did I get so lucky?"

"Just by being you," I said firmly. I kissed his mouth and felt the tickle of stubble against mine. I could happily gobble him up right here and now in front of everybody. Literally. And have a fucking good time doing it.

He kissed me back, then sat with his nose lightly touching mine. "What if Abbie doesn't want me as much as she wants you and the other guys?"

"She does," I said with certainty. "I can guarantee you one million percent that she wouldn't suck your cock if she didn't want you as much as the rest of us."

She was as invested in this as I was. As all the rest of the guys were. I knew she wouldn't fuck any of us if what she felt for them wasn't strong and genuine.

"Would you like me to give you some time alone with her when we get a chance?" I offered.

His brow creased and smoothed out in thought. Finally, he shook his head. "No. I mean, yeah I'd like to keep having one-on-one conversations with her. But you mean a date with just her and I, right? I kinda like it being the three of us. I'd feel like I'm cheating otherwise."

"Me too," I agreed. We'd been a duo for so long, it felt right to keep doing that.

"She's something special, isn't she?" he asked. "We shared a lot of women but no one has ever felt like…" He exhaled. "Like home. You know? Like you do."

"I do know," I agreed. "I feel the same way about you and her. We're just a trio of comfy throw pillows, or a blanket. Sexier than that though."

He chuckled. His breath brushed my lips. "I don't know, I've seen some pretty sexy throw pillows."

"Did we just enter an episode of confessions from

teenage Channing?" I teased. "Did you used to hump pillows?"

He laughed again. "Didn't everyone?"

"No," I said. "But I did have this big plush elephant I got close to." I loved that elephant. The social worker who drove me to one of my foster homes gave it to me. I took it to the next two before the third one wouldn't allow it. Apparently it was too old and manky by then. That was the excuse I was given.

I left it behind with a younger girl who probably needed it more than I did anyway.

The first time I got any royalties from the band, I tracked down a similar plush elephant and bought it. It sits on my couch in my living room, taking up space. And not getting humped.

Channing must have seen how sad I got thinking about my past. He cupped my cheeks with his hands and slanted his mouth over mine. He kissed me, slow and deep and loving. It washed away every last bit of self-doubt the conversation gave me.

You love both of them, the voice in the back of my head said. I put all of that emotion into my kiss so Channing would know and feel it, but I wouldn't be ready to tell Abbie that for a while yet. We'd get there when the time was right, but that time was not right now.

If not now, then when? The back of my mind asked. I didn't have the answer to that. I would know when I knew.

I hoped our conversation put Channing's fears to rest. All I wanted was for everyone to be happy, whatever it took to get us there.

17

ABBIE

"I'M NEVER DRINKING BEER AGAIN," Asher declared. He lay down on the floor backstage and groaned.

"Sure you're not." Penn flopped down into a chair. "Until next time."

Asher groaned again. "Don't talk so loud." He pressed his hands to either side of his forehead.

"Poor baby." I stretched out beside him. "I thought you took something for the pain?"

"I did. It hasn't worked yet." He lowered one hand and started to trace circles around my upper arm.

Zeke sat beside us. "If you think he's bad now, you should see him when he gets sick. He gets the worst case of man flu I've ever seen."

"I do not," Asher protested, his voice full of discomfort. "I just get sicker than everyone else."

"Bullshit," Penn said. "You bitch and moan louder than anyone else. Anyone would think you are dying the way you carry on sometimes."

"I'm dying right now," Asher said. "Tell Blazing Violet when they go on not to play too loud, would you?"

"We could ask Danny to play in your place?" Tully suggested. "You can stay here and get some sleep."

"I thought you were supposed to get more seasoned as you got older?" Landon said to Channing. "You'd think at Asher's age—"

"I'm not old," Asher protested. He picked up his head. "Why aren't the rest of you hung over too?"

"Who said we're not?" I asked.

"I'm not," Penn said. "I only had one beer."

"I don't get hangovers," Zeke said with a shrug. He hadn't really drank that much either. Honestly, neither had I. It was difficult to let loose with the evil twins lurking around, ready to take advantage of it.

"By the way, I'll be fine to go on stage," Asher said. Evidently it took time for the words to filter into his brain.

"If you don't puke while you're out there," Penn said helpfully.

Asher grunted. "Don't talk about puke."

"Okay." Penn shrugged. "I won't mention chunks of carrot or corn. Or green mush." He smiled slyly.

"You fucking suck," Asher told him. "If I spew, I'm going to spew on you." He rolled over as though he was about to do just that.

Penn shot up out of his chair and moved to the other side of the room. "The hell you are!"

Landon chuckled and lowered himself down beside me. He lay propped up on his elbow. "You know what would be nice?"

Channing sat down beside him. "If Asher stopped complaining?"

"Thanks for the sympathy, guys," Asher said sarcastically.

"What would be nice?" I asked Landon. I wasn't going to give Asher any sympathy. Hangovers were one hundred percent self-inflicted. He didn't have to accept when that German guy challenged him to a drinking challenge. We were lucky he didn't pass out on the floor.

"A big comfortable nest," Landon said. "A bunch of pillows, blankets, stuff like that. Somewhere we could all have a nap while we wait to go on stage."

"Fuck yes," Channing said. "Maybe a big-screen TV and a movie."

"And a big juicy steak," Zeke said, deliberately

speaking in Asher's direction. "The kind dripping with pan juices. And some fresh vegetables on the side. And chips, of course. You have to have hot chips with your steak."

"I thought you loved me," Asher groaned. "If you keep talking about food, I'm going to hurl."

"You might feel better if you do," Tully said. "Get the rest of it out of your system."

"I tried that twice already, it didn't help." Asher rolled over and pressed his forehead to the floor.

I exchanged glances with Landon, shook my head and smiled. "I guess he won't be drinking again."

"He will." Landon started to trace little circles over the bare skin between my chin and the neckline of my dress. "He's like this every time. In a couple of hours, he'll be ready to drink more than he drank last night."

"No way," Asher said, his voice muffled by the floor. "Never again."

Landon's circles got a little lower, until the tip of his finger slipped under the fabric.

I started to melt, although his touch was feather-light.

"You like that?" he whispered.

"Yeah, I do," I whispered back. In spite of the fact we were in a room where anyone might walk in, or maybe because of it, my pussy started to throb. When had I become such a risk taker? It was a recent thing, since I'd met them. They brought out my inner sex goddess.

"Good." He peeled back the fabric of my dress and the cup of my bra, letting a blast of cool air tickle my nipple. He quickly covered it with his mouth, sucking gently on my sensitive peak.

I closed my eyes, only opening them again for a moment when Channing did the same to my other breast. They really were one hell of a team.

"Can anyone join this party?" Tully asked. The other guys must have agreed, because the guitarist gently bent my knees and knelt down between them. He hooked his fingers into the gusset of my panties and pushed them aside. He lowered his face between my thighs and started to tease my pussy with his tongue.

Between the three of them, I was shivering and shuddering in moments.

The first notes of Blazing Violet's music echoed through the corridor and into the room.

Tully strummed me as Blaise strummed his guitar, starting slow but building quickly, driving the audience into a frenzy. Tully sucked my clit and thrust his tongue into me and around my folds. He lapped at me like a man dying of thirst. And I was the only well in sight.

Blood thundered through me to the beat of Danny's drums and Ryan's bass. The tempo increased, pounding around the stadium and right into my core.

I shattered into a million pieces. I arched my back and rocked against Tully's mouth. Violet held a high note that matched mine, long and intense until my breath was gone from my body.

I flopped down, gasping, as the song ended and another began.

Tully, his face glistening, moved up my body to the beat of the music, grooving as he went. He undid the front of his jeans, his eyes on me, searching for my reaction. For my consent to do this here.

I gave all of that and more with a long, lingering look laced with heat.

He nodded and pushed his jeans down just enough to free his erection.

Landon and Channing didn't stop lavishing attention on my breasts. They too moved in time with Blazing Violet's music, sucking and licking faster and slower with the tempo.

Tully positioned himself outside my pussy and slid inside during a long bridge. He let out a deep, low groan of pleasure that matched the cry of Blaise's guitar.

"You feel so fucking incredible." He was careful, as always, letting me get used to him note by note, before he slid all the way, balls deep, into my body.

"So do you," I said. When he started to thrust, my hips rose and fell in perfect harmony to meet each one.

Zeke abandoned his chair and came to sit beside us, eyes dark with desire. He glanced at us both before he slipped a hand under Tully's stomach and started to circle my clit with his fingertips.

I gasped, overwhelmed by the barrage of sensations from all four guys, and the pounding music from above. It was like the club Landon took us too, but more personal somehow. We knew the set Blazing Violet would play, and all the lyrics, all the notes. That became the soundtrack for this moment.

Four became five as Asher, apparently feeling well enough already, rolled over and opened the front of Zeke's jeans. He helped the singer's cock to pop free and lowered his mouth onto him.

"Holy crap, yeah," Zeke breathed. "Your mouth is incredible, babe. Don't stop doing that."

Apparently not wanting to be left out, Penn moved over, suspicious eyes on Asher until he knelt next to me. He leaned all the way over and kissed my mouth, all lips and teeth. He fucked my mouth with his tongue until I was breathless.

I reached the edge of the precipice again and hurtled over, unable to stop myself, even if Penn ordered me to. The blood rushing through my ears was louder than the pounding of the drums that poured through the speakers. It surged all the way through me lifting me up and dragging me down until every nerve in my body was screaming with pure joy.

My orgasm claimed Tully. My body convulsed around him until he came as well. He shouted a pure note of pleasure. He pounded frantically, then stilled and ground into me, my pussy milking him for every drop.

Zeke was close behind, thrusting frantically into Asher's mouth.

Watching his face scrunch up in concentration, his mouth open as he gasped and panted, then exhaled as he came, made me come again.

This time was even more intense and all-encompassing than before. If I thought all my nerves felt it the second time, I was wrong. This one, I swear I felt down at the end of my hair and into my toenails.

I screamed, this time in time with Sharkey's

keyboard, backed by Ryan's bass. Danny's drums came back in as I hit my peak, driving me higher. I crashed down as he clashed his cymbals, ending the song to a storm of applause.

When I finally came down, I was floppy, bone-less, panting.

Tully slid out of me and Landon took his place. At the same time, Channing positioned himself so he could slide his cock into Landon's mouth.

Inspired, Penn undid the front of his jeans and slid his cock into my mouth.

Zeke rolled Asher over the other way and did the same to him. It wasn't for the music on the stage, all anyone would hear was the sound of sucking and groaning.

"Thank you!" Violet shouted. "This next song is dedicated to a guy I once knew. It's called 'Blow Your Top.'"

I snorted with the irony of us blowing to this song, and went on sucking.

Landon grinned and thrust faster and faster into my body, while Penn matched him stroke for stroke.

I sucked and teased him with my tongue, ran my hand up and down from my chin to his balls. Out of the corner of my eye, I watched the other guys. What was it about watching a guy blow off another guy that was as hot as fuck? Maybe because they were so big and masculine, but like this they were vulnerable and giving.

Or maybe I just had a thing for stubble and cocks. I mean, both of those were good things too.

I don't know if Penn agreed, but he fixed his gaze on my face and came next, flooding my mouth with hot, pearly cum. He looked expectant and slowly slid his cock out from between my lips. He arched an eyebrow at me.

My mouth closed, I smiled and swallowed deliberately.

"Fuck yeah," he said softly. "You are fucking next level, woman."

"Hell yeah I am," I said with a grin. "And you're delicious."

He groaned in appreciation.

Landon, Channing and Asher were thrusting at about the same speed. I knew all three were close to coming. I looked over at Penn meaningfully. If he could be the conductor for me…

He sat back on his haunches and nodded. "Asher, don't come yet."

Asher groaned. "But I want to."

"Yeah," Penn said, "but wait."

Asher moaned in protest, but slowed down

slightly.

Zeke raised his eyebrows, but went on sucking.

"You two are close aren't you?" Penn asked Landon and Channing. "Yep, I thought so. That's it, go right to the edge."

"Asher?"

Asher made an indeterminate noise.

"Abbie wants you to come now. All of you."

Whether it was his intention or not, but when all three guys came, I came for a fourth time. This time it was so hard and intense I went all the way to infinity, stayed there for approximately a decade, then gradually floated back down through the atmosphere and back into my body.

The guys all flopped down on the floor around me, panting ruggedly and sighing.

Blazing Violet was in approximately the middle of their set.

Shit.

I was going to need to clean up and change my panties before I went on stage after them.

I barely registered Jackson sticking his head through the door, clearing his throat and then hurrying away.

Poor guy, the things he saw while just doing his job.

18

ABBIE

"So... About before..."

I managed to get through my set with my knees a little weak. If I wasn't sweaty before I went under the hot lights, I was sweaty after. Thankfully the audience was receptive, with none of the attitude of the guy from the Q and A. They even shouted for an encore before I left the stage. They cheered again when I went back to sing with the guys.

By the time I was done, I was itching for a shower.

I didn't get far before I almost bumped into Jackson, who was pacing back and forth outside the green room.

He stopped to look at me, and waved a hand back and forth in the air.

"Don't worry about it," he said. "Still not the worst thing I've ever seen." And yet he couldn't meet my eyes.

"I just—" I needed to say something, if only to know we were okay after what he saw. "We didn't plan for any of that. It just happened. If we stopped to think about it for half a second, it might not have."

Jackson sighed and leaned against the wall, one knee bent, the bottom of his shoe pressed against the white painted brick. He crossed his arms over his chest and lowered his head for a moment.

When he looked back up he said, "I'm not in the business of telling any of you where you should and shouldn't, you know…"

"Fuck?" I asked.

He winced. "Yeah. But I could have been anyone. Press get past security. Fans get past security. Hell, it might have been a security officer with a phone, who decided the photo would make them more money than their job does. There's only so much damage control I, or the label, could do if a photo like that leaked. You'd be looking at one hell of a shitstorm."

He glanced at my chest, then quickly up to my face. He'd obviously seen my bare breasts and was trying not to think about them too much. He also might have seen Landon's ass, but for the most part we kept our clothes on. That in itself was pretty amazing given everything that went on.

"I'm sorry," I said sincerely. "The last thing we want to do is create a shitstorm."

"Next time, maybe close the door," he suggested. He scrubbed a hand over his chin. "I feel like I'm talking about a group of teenagers. I know you're not that. I just don't want any of you doing anything you'll all regret."

"Taking care of our image is your job," I pointed out. "I think you're within your rights to yell at us." I didn't regret a moment of it, but he was right about closing the door. Or at least, posting a security guard we could trust outside.

Although, wouldn't that defeat the purpose? The possibility of being caught was part of the fun.

"Do you want me to yell at you?" Judging by the way he swallowed, that wasn't what he wanted to do with me.

That realisation made me swallow too. I liked Jackson a lot. He was the island of calm in a sea of crazy, even though we razzed him relentlessly. Did I think of him like another boyfriend? Would he want that? Would the rest of the guys?

All of those questions had my head spinning.

I completely understood why he kept his feelings

under wraps until now. I'd told Zeke, Asher and Tully I loved them, and when the time was right I would tell the other three. Getting involved with me would be complicated for him. And an extra complication for all of us. Not to mention what happened the last time I got involved with anyone who worked for my label and was older than me. Jackson was at least a decade older.

Not that I was worried about the age gap. That was a tiny concern in the grand scheme of things.

"Actually, I'd prefer it if you didn't yell at me," I said. "Unless you're cheering me on."

"I will never *not* cheer you on," he said softly. "I'm in the top seven of your biggest supporters. Top eight if you count Levi."

"I hope I can count the boss in that number," I said lightly. My bank account was looking a lot healthier these days and no doubt so was his. Not that he was short on a dollar or two to start with.

"Definitely." Jackson nodded firmly. "He always speaks highly of you. As do I."

"That goes both ways," I said. "You two have been amazing. I couldn't have asked for better support. It's made a world of difference." I stood on my toes and lightly kissed his cheek.

He watched me with his denim blue eyes. I got

the impression he was tempted to turn his face to meet my lips with his.

I was tempted to kiss his mouth and see how he tasted.

I stepped back and gave him an awkward smile.

He responded with a matching one. "Were you on your way to the shower?" he asked. "Would you like me to come with you?"

He realised what he said and his face turned pink.

My mouth went dry. Apparently after four orgasms, there was room for more. His suggestion, however innocently intended, sent a shockwave of heat through my body.

He cleared his throat loudly. "I mean, I can escort you there and wait outside to make sure no evil twins turn up."

"Right," I said. "Of course. I'd like that." Hopefully stadium security was good enough to keep out Hunter and Parker, but if anyone could slip in, they could.

"Thank you. I'd feel safer with you nearby."

We stood awkwardly for a moment or two before he gestured towards the locker rooms with a grimace.

The downside to playing in stadiums which often housed professional sporting teams was that the locker rooms smelled like old socks and sweaty feet. It was the least sexy smell ever. Maybe that wasn't such a bad thing under the circumstances.

I took my change of clothes and a towel and stepped into the cubicle. If it was one of the other guys, there wouldn't have been any question as to whether or not I should close the door, much less lock it. I trusted Jackson not to try anything with me, but it might be better to be naked out of sight.

For now. Things between us were awkward enough already.

And confusing. There was no doubt in my mind I cared about him. I couldn't imagine not having him in my life, one way or another. Would taking things a step further ruin things between us? Worse than that, would it ruin things between Jackson and the other guys? If I thought it would, then friendship would be as far as it could ever go.

Fuck, why couldn't my life be simple for a change? Apparently I thrived on chaos and hot guys. Of course that got me to wondering what Jackson looked like under his clothes. I'd never seen him with his shirt off. That didn't seem fair now that he'd seen me without one.

I shook my head to myself, stripped and left my

sweaty clothes on the floor before I stepped into the warm flow of the shower.

It was strange how quickly I got used to sharing with someone else. These days, when I washed, I usually had at least one of the guys with me. We always did more than get clean, of course. Any time I was naked was an opportunity for touching and orgasms. I certainly couldn't complain about that.

About halfway through, I heard Jackson talking to someone. I couldn't hear the words; his voice was low, but he sounded agitated. Was that because of our conversation or had something else happened? Who was he talking to? I couldn't hear anyone else, so he must be on his phone.

I listened for a moment and decided he didn't sound panicked, just cranky.

I squeezed out shampoo onto my palm and started to wash my hair. Partly because I needed to and partly so I couldn't hear what he was saying. Chances were, it was about work and was none of my business. We weren't the only ones he managed.

"No," he was saying as I rinsed my hair. "Not gonna happen." He spoke in a frustrated growl. "Just —no. I haven't been able to…" His voice dropped off lower again.

I felt bad for overhearing even that little. I rinsed

my hair for longer than I needed to, so my ears were under the water.

Finally, when I couldn't stay there any longer because I'd look like a prune, I turned off the water. The locker room fell into silence.

Jackson must have ended his phone call.

I dried quickly and got dressed in a clean T-shirt and track pants. And yes, dry panties. For now.

I grabbed my sweaty clothes off the floor and opened the door.

Just as I expected, Jackson was alone, leaning against the wall on the other side of the locker room. His mouth was set in a firm line like it was when he was annoyed.

"Is everything okay?" I asked. "I thought I heard you talking to someone." I quickly added, "I'm sorry, it's none of my business."

"No, it's okay." He rubbed the back of his neck. "Nothing to worry about, just work." Once again, he wouldn't meet my eyes. Was that because of the phone call or our awkward conversation from before?

"Okay, if you're sure," I said.

He pushed himself off the wall. "I'm sure. Let's go listen to the guys' last few songs. Last concert of the European leg."

After this, we had a couple of days off before travelling to North America.

Personally, I was looking forward to the small break. A tour this long was exhausting. If we didn't get a few days to rest, we'd be incoherent by the end of it.

Assuming we were coherent at the start of it. I liked to think we were, more or less.

"Let's do it," I said without thinking.

Now it was my turn for my face to heat.

"I mean, listen to them." I seemed to have sex on the brain these days. Which wasn't usually a bad thing, but it might get me into trouble if I didn't watch my mouth. Maybe I shouldn't think about my mouth, because then I might think about what I could do to him with it. That could lead down a rabbit hole I wasn't ready to jump into yet.

"I thought that was what you meant," he said. He gave me a smile but I suspected he wished I meant the other kind of 'do it'. The bulge in his pants when I lowered my gaze slightly confirmed that suspicion.

That he wasn't going to pressure me was obvious. I appreciated that. I didn't know where this would go, if anywhere, but I wanted to take my time.

He opened the door that led out of the locker rooms and gestured for me to step out first.

I was approximately a thousand percent certain he wanted to grab me and kiss me, but he didn't. He just waited until I stepped past and closed the door behind us.

"So that's how it's done?" I asked, trying to lighten the mood.

He looked at me funny before he realised what I was trying to say. "Yes, that's how you close the door. Should I demonstrate a few times so you know how to do it yourself if I'm not around?" He grinned and even gave me a wink.

I tried to ignore the way my heart flipped.

"That's not necessary," I said with a laugh. "Your demonstration was more than adequate. But if I can't do it by myself next time, I have you on speed dial."

He laughed and put a hand on my lower back as we walked back in the direction of the stage.

19

ABBIE

"So, something happened…kinda," I started slowly.

Zeke and Asher both stopped with a piece of strudel a couple of centimetres from their mouths. Lucky for them I hadn't waited until they'd shoved them in.

Zeke lowered his strudel and put it back on his plate. He rubbed his thumb over his fingers to dust off flakes of pastry. "Who do I have to beat up?"

Asher bit into his strudel, and nodded. "Same question," he said with a full mouth. "Just say the word and I'm there."

"That's very touching," I said dryly. "You don't have to beat anyone up. I don't think so anyway."

This wasn't going how I planned. I rehearsed

every word in my head several times, but none of them came out the way I wanted.

"Is everything all right?" Landon asked gently. He touched the tips of his fingers to my wrist and gave me a worried look.

Channing, who sat on the other side of him, looked like he was ready to join Zeke and Asher in pounding the crap out of anyone I wanted them to.

"Yes," I said quickly. "Everything's fine. I..." I might as well jump straight in and tell them. "I think Jackson has a thing for me."

Asher sounded like he was about to choke on his strudel. He coughed a couple of times before he grabbed his coffee and took a gulp or two. "Ahh, fuck, hot."

Penn snorted a laugh at him. "You're such a dork."

"Love you too," Asher muttered.

Zeke patted Asher on the back until he was composed again. Once it was apparent the drummer wasn't going to choke and die, and hadn't scalded his mouth, Zeke turned back to me.

"Are you sure?"

"No," I admitted. "I mean, kinda. Maybe it was just his reaction to seeing us all together before the concert."

"That'll make anyone horny," Tully said.

"Makes me horny just thinking about it," Landon said.

"Most things make you horny," Channing told him.

Landon grinned. "That's true. Life is too short not to enjoy every minute of it."

"Anyway," Zeke drawled, "it wouldn't surprise me. How could anyone not have a thing for you?"

"What Zeke said," Asher said.

"I third that," Tully said.

"Yeah," Penn agreed.

"What do you want to do about it?" Zeke asked carefully.

"I don't know," I admitted. "I know I don't want to mess things up between you and him and him and I. If he becomes a part of this, it will change things."

"Like, we won't be able to tease him anymore?" Asher pouted.

"As if you're going to stop giving him shit," Penn scoffed.

"That's true," Asher agreed, more cheerful now. "Jackson is like a big brother to us, so it wouldn't be that weird."

"No weirder than this already is," Penn said.

"So you're okay with whatever happens?" I asked tentatively.

"Totally," Zeke said with a shrug. "It's not like we're talking about the evil twins here. We know Jackson and trust him and he knows all our shit. He's practically one of us anyway."

"What if it turns out badly?" I asked. That was hands down my biggest fear. This could so easily go all kinds of sideways.

"What if it turns out badly with any of us?" Zeke gestured around the table. Technically, three tables. The small café in Frankfurt didn't have a table big enough for us all to sit at, so we'd dragged them together. Fortunately, the staff hadn't seemed to mind. Especially after the guys agreed to take selfies with all of them.

A little bit of good will goes a long way.

"That would be bad," Asher said. "We only have to see how Violet and Blaise are to know how messy it is working with someone you hate."

"They don't hate each other," Tully said. "They just haven't figured that out yet."

"Besides, it's possible to work with somebody you can't stand," Penn said. He looked meaningfully at Asher.

Asher flipped him off. "You say you can't stand me, but I know otherwise. I'm way too adorable for that."

"Keep telling yourself that," Penn said. "Everyone knows I'm the adorable one." He pretended to fluff the back of his hair.

"You're all adorable," I said. "So much so I can't even stand it sometimes."

Jackson was adorable too.

Honestly, I shouldn't have been surprised at the guy's reactions. They'd all been very accepting of the situation so far. More than a lot of other guys would be.

"That explains the vibes I was getting from Jackson," Asher said thoughtfully. "I don't know why I didn't see it sooner. Now I think about it, it was pretty fucking obvious. He clearly adores you as much as we do."

"I'm relieved we don't have to beat anyone up," Zeke said.

Channing made a face like he was disappointed he wouldn't get the chance. No doubt something would come up sooner or later.

"Can I ask you something?" Landon asked softly.

"Of course," I said. "Anything." At this point, I had nothing left to hide, or that I would want to avoid talking about. Not that I could think of anyway.

"If you want to be with Jackson, what does that

mean for the rest of us?" His eyes were a silent plea for me to be honest.

I understood why he was asking. It might be easy to assume I would either be with Jackson or with Wolf Venom.

I put a hand lightly on his cheek. "I'm not going to choose Jackson instead of you guys. He'd have to be part of this big crazy group, or not at all."

It was that simple. Every single one of these guys held a bit of my heart and that was how I wanted it. I couldn't imagine anything they would do that would make me walk away from them. We were a team, a family.

"You're not getting rid of me that easily," I added.

He smiled in relief and kissed my mouth.

"Good, because we don't want to get rid of you," Landon said. He turned to the rest of the guys. "Do we?"

"Hell no," Zeke and Asher said in unison.

"No way," Channing said.

"Nope," Penn agreed.

"Not a chance," Tully said.

I couldn't help but feel all warm and fuzzy inside. They really were basically the best guys ever.

"I guess I'll have a conversation with Jackson when I get a chance," I said slowly. "Talk about whether I was picking up on the wrong vibes or not." For all I knew, he was caught up in the moment, nothing more.

"Speak of the devil," Penn said.

I flinched, immediately assuming he meant the evil twins, who Zeke had mentioned a couple of minutes ago. If they brazenly walked into the same café we were sitting in…

"Hey." It wasn't the evil twins. It wasn't even Jackson. It was Levi, who grabbed a chair from another table and dragged it over. He sat down next to Tully. "You don't mind if I join you, do you? Good. Mr Cole, I wanted to speak to you about something."

"Yes, Mr Jones," Tully said with a smile. "This is all very formal. Am I in trouble?"

"Should you be?" Levi asked. He rested his elbow on the table and propped up his cheek with his fingertips. At the same time, he raised his eyebrow at Tully.

"Probably." Tully shrugged. "But if I am, then everyone else at the table should too."

"Did you just throw us under the bus?" Asher asked.

"Do you have a guilty conscience?" Tully cocked his head at the drummer.

"Not this week," Asher said lightly. "Anyway, I believe Levi wanted to talk to *you.*"

"Yes I do," Levi agreed. "I was hoping to discuss a merger between White Wolf Records and Onyx Riot Records."

"Ohhh, are we talking about a hostile takeover?" Asher asked eagerly.

"Hopefully not," Levi said. "There's no reason for things to get hostile." He turned back to Tully. "When you get back to Australia, look through all of the records, have an accountant look over everything. I think you'll probably find Onyx Riot is a fucking mess. To put it politely. I'd like to help put it back together. Or absorb its assets into White Wolf, assuming it has any assets left. There are some good staff, producers and acts left attached to them. I think you'll agree it's best not to leave people hanging when their livelihoods are at stake."

Tully nodded. "I agree one hundred percent. They don't deserve what mess Pete left behind. I don't need to talk to an accountant and look over the books. I trust you. I'm in." He stuck out his hand to Levi. Honestly, he looked relieved. I suspected he hadn't wanted to deal with the running of the label, at least not yet.

Levi shook it, but said, "Even if you do trust me,

don't sign on the dotted line until you've had a third party look it over. I won't be. But I think between us we can put something together that will help everyone. Especially our bank accounts."

"As if either of you need more money," Asher said.

"Someone has to pay for you to fly around the world and put on concerts," Levi said. "I hate to break it to you, but that money doesn't come out of thin air."

Asher stared at him. "What? It doesn't? Well shit." He shook his head in mock disbelief.

We all laughed.

"Would either of you mind if I sit in on some of that?" I asked. "I'd feel better knowing Onyx Riot was being run the way it should be."

"Are you going to hook up with Levi too?" Penn asked. He narrowed his eyes at the label's owner, then at me.

Levi and I both looked at him in surprise but Levi laughed.

"My girlfriend might not approve of that," he said.

Asher's mouth dropped open. "You have a girlfriend? Since when?"

"Since it's none of your business," Levi retorted. "I

don't ask about your love life and you don't get to ask about mine." He propped his cheek on the opposite hand.

"As if saying that is going to deter Asher," Penn said.

"I can try, can't I?" Levi shrugged.

"You can try," Asher agreed. "But Penn is right. If you won't tell me, I'll ask Jackson. I bet he knows. Doesn't he?"

Levi looked back at Tully. "I think the first thing we need to do is buy those drum machines we were talking about."

Asher held up his hands. "Okay, okay. I'll be good. You're as big a spoilsport as Jackson." He pouted and pretended to look a lot more offended than he actually was.

"Yes I am," Levi agreed cheerfully. "Don't you forget it." He waggled his finger under Asher's nose.

Zeke slung an arm over Asher's shoulders. "Don't worry, I won't let them replace you with the machine. If they do that, I'll walk."

We all knew that was an idle threat, but if Zeke left, there would be no band, not really.

"That's sweet." Asher kissed his mouth, then pressed his nose to Zeke's.

"You're sweet," Zeke told him.

"Fuck," Penn said. "You two are going to rot my teeth." He grimaced at them both.

They turned to him and smiled unashamedly. Zeke put an arm around my shoulder and pulled me over so the three of us were cheek to cheek to cheek. "How's this for sweet?"

Penn snorted. "Abbie is the only sweet one."

I batted my eyelashes. "So are you." I put an arm around Landon to pull him in too. He brought Channing in with him.

"We're all sweet," I declared.

"I don't know why you want to know about my love life when you have all of this in front of you," Levi said to Asher.

"I'm a hopeless romantic," Asher said.

"You're half right," Penn teased.

"Fine," Asher said with a shrug. "I am a romantic."

That obviously wasn't what Penn was implying, but for once he didn't point it out.

20

ABBIE

"So, you think I'm sweet, huh?" Penn slipped his hand into mine as we stepped out of the café and started back to the hotel.

"You have your moments," I said teasingly. I smiled up at him. He was so good looking he made my breath catch in my throat. Good looking and mine.

He pouted playfully. "I have lots of moments. Some more memorable than others."

"Like your ability to orchestrate four orgasms at once? " I let go of his hand and slipped my arm around him so I could snuggle as we walked. "Those are some mad skills."

He slipped his arm around me too. "It's not rocket science. It's about watching for the signs someone is about to come. Anyone could do it if they paid enough attention."

"Maybe," I said slowly. "But there's a knack to ordering people to wait as well. Not everyone has the right tone of voice for it. I don't think I do."

"No, I don't think you do either," he agreed, much to my surprise. Fortunately, he added, "Not because you aren't as bossy as me, but because your voice makes me want to come. I couldn't stop myself."

"So…" I thought about that for a moment. "I could potentially make you come on command?"

He leaned down to nestle his face in my hair. "Sweetheart, you could potentially make me do whatever you want. I was determined to hate your guts when we met and now—"

"Now you like my guts?" I finished for him.

"I love your guts," he said softly. "I love your everything. I love *you*."

A flush of warm emotion rushed through me, making my heart sing with unfiltered happiness.

"I love you too." It was a relief to tell him that. For a long time I was worried he would keep hating me, and wanting me off the tour. Not that long ago, he would have agreed with that asshole at the Q and A. Hell, he would have *been* that asshole.

Or at least, he would have *claimed* to think that way.

He must have cottoned on to what I was thinking, because he said, "I'm sorry for being such a prick back then. I'm a temperamental asshole, as anyone will tell you. I wanted you the moment I laid eyes on you. Not just physically but like this, an actual relationship. That scared the shit out of me, and I took it out on you. Plus, to some extent, I was scared the audiences would love you more than they love us. The idea of you stealing the show pissed me off."

"I understand how that would frustrate you," I said. I'd be pissed if that happened to me, but I liked hearing him admit he cared about me the whole time. That made me feel warm and fuzzy inside. "And now?"

"And now," he said slowly, "you compliment the show. You're a part of it and we all stand out. The tour is better for having you on it."

For some reason, I felt tears prickle in my eyes. "See, I said you were sweet."

"Yeah, well." His shoulders twitched. "I still would have been pissed off if you stole my solo."

I blinked away tears in time to see him grin. "Of course you would, because you're a brat." I pressed my shoulder into his chest.

"Hell yeah I am," he agreed. "Always have been, always will be."

"I don't think I've ever heard anyone say they're proud to be a brat before," I said. "Dickhead, asshole, jerk, twat, but never brat."

His chest rumbled against my arm as he laughed. "Firstly, more people should be proud of being a brat. Secondly, who do you know who is proud of being a twat?"

I thought for a moment. "Yeah, okay I don't know. I'm sure there's someone. By the way, I forgive you for being a dickhead when we first met. You kept me on my toes, but I can't expect everyone to like me."

"Believe it or not, neither can I," he said. "I know, that's hard to get your head around. I'm such a like-able guy." He gave me a self deprecating smile.

"I think you are," I said. "You're honest and funny, and sarcasm is a sign of intelligence."

"I must be fucking brilliant then," he said with a laugh.

"You're a musical genius," I pointed out. He was definitely a smart guy, and educated. He had an interesting vocabulary of insults ready to dish out as needed. What more could anyone want?

He groaned softly. "Yeah, that was my parents'

weapon of choice in getting me to do what they wanted."

He put on a high pitched voice and said, "*Beau, you're a prodigy. You owe it to yourself to take full advantage of the gifts you've been given. To yourself and the whole wide world.*" He stretched out an arm.

"A big chunk of the whole wide world loves your gifts," I pointed out. "Your parents don't?"

"They hate what I'm doing," he admitted. "When they introduce me to their friends, they refer to me as, 'our son who dabbles in music these days.' As if I sit in the lounge room playing the triangle."

"Ouch." I winced on his behalf. "If I was your mother, I would be proud of you. You're an amazing guy and you've done incredible things. Even without the band, you were destined to."

"You think so?" He glanced over at me.

It was the first time I ever heard him sound insecure.

"I absolutely think so," I said firmly. "A lot of people would have walked away from music if they were pressured into it." I sighed and added, "My parents wanted me to get a normal nine-to-five job. I don't think they cared if I worked in a bank or as a teacher, or if I washed dogs for a living, as long as I wasn't doing something that wouldn't guarantee me a regular income."

"Of course, you became a singer," he said. "The definition of irregular income."

"They were disappointed, but they supported me." I slipped my hand into his back pocket. His ass was warm through the fabric of his jeans. "I think they hoped it was a phase and I would get past it some day."

"If they're anything like mine, they would have been...ecstatic isn't the word. When Onyx Riot Records broke your contract, they must've hoped that meant you would do what they wanted?" He cocked his head at me, his expression interested and attentive.

"Something like that," I agreed. "They kept saying unsubtle things like, 'Now you're not singing anymore,' like I could just turn it off like a tap. I don't think they were impressed when Levi approached me. They were pissed after what Vance and Pete both did and they wanted to protect me I guess."

"Seems like a theme around here," Penn said. "All any of us wants to do is protect you. Truth is, you're a badass. For the most part, you don't need protection from the big bad world." He gave me such a gentle, loving smile my heart did a triple flip and landed in a half melted puddle in my chest. He was so fucking sweet and gorgeous, even if he wouldn't admit to it. Deep down, he was as much a romantic as Asher.

"Just the evil twins," I said. "And people like them."

"We all need protection against them," he agreed. "Even I couldn't deal with them alone. Little assholes." His tone was begrudging. Rightfully so.

"We all take care of each other," I said. "I think it's safe to say we always support what everyone does. We certainly won't be disappointed with each other's choice of career."

He snorted a laugh. "Definitely not. We'd be hypocrites if we did."

We walked in silence for a couple of minutes, lost in our own thoughts and taking comfort in each other.

He was the one who broke the silence. "What do you think is going to come after the tour? You're not going to give up your career for us, are you?"

"You wouldn't want me to?" I stepped around a discarded pizza box and looked up at him.

"For us? No. Not until you're ready to do that, and you're not. You're taking off again and I, for one, will not be responsible for clipping your wings. No more than you would do to me or any of the guys."

"No, I don't want to do that," I agreed. "And you're right, I'm not ready to step away yet. From my career or you guys."

"I guess," I said slowly, "we spend as much time with each other as we can while none of us are on tour, and video chat a shit ton when we are. If we want this to work badly enough, we'll find a way." We had to. I knew the guys wanted this as much as I did. It wouldn't be easy, I knew that too, but it would be worth it to be together.

"Maybe I should buy you a chastity belt for when you're on tour by yourself," he said jokingly. "The kind you can only unlock with the key, which I'll keep."

I nudged him with my elbow. "What if Jackson and I go on tour without you guys?"

"Then I'll get a chastity belt for him too." Penn grinned.

"You really are a brat," I said with a laugh. "But in case there is any doubt, I would never cheat on you guys. In order for this to work, we need to communicate. And we will."

"And we'll fly out and see each other as much as we can," he said. "Whatever it takes."

He paused for a moment and grimaced.

"What?" I asked.

"I don't like the idea of not seeing you every day," he admitted. "You might be a pain in the ass, but you're my pain in the ass and I'm used to you being around. I like having you nearby, or next to me. On top of me. Or underneath me. Or on your knees in front of me. Or…"

I laughed. "Yeah, I get it. Just like you're my asshole and I like having you around."

"And they say romance is dead," he joked. He kissed my hair. "I love you so much."

"I love you so much too," I said. "I don't think we would be us if we didn't rib each other mercilessly."

"That's true, we wouldn't," he agreed.

"That's how I know you and Asher really like each other," I said. I glanced over my shoulder to where the drummer was walking hand-in-hand with Zeke. "Because you give each other hell."

"Yeah, Penn is okay," Asher said. "Even though I want to punch him in the cock every once in a while."

"Back at you, bro," Penn told him. To me, he said, "Yeah, we give each other shit but we never mean anything by it. It's just our twisted sense of humour. Or as I like to say, part of my charm." He put a hand under his chin and smiled.

"Absolutely," I agreed. A little bit of razzing

between brothers was okay as long as they didn't get personal and nasty. They all seemed to know where the line was and not to cross it. Their unity was a big part of their success. And yes, part of their charm.

"So," I started, slowly and carefully as though I was about to ask something difficult or awkward, "if you didn't play the triangle in the living room, then where did you play it?"

Penn laughed. "In the conservatory, of course. Where I played all my music. And before you ask, yes, I can play a fucking good tune on the triangle. Remind me to show you sometime."

"I will," I said. If anyone could make such a simple instrument sound incredible, it would be Penn.

21

LANDON

"You feeling better about everything?" Channing pulled my legs over his lap and started to take off my shoes and socks. He was the only person I knew who didn't seem to be grossed out by feet. Specifically feet which were encased in hot socks and shoes for hours.

Or maybe it was just my feet he didn't mind.

When they were bare, he started to massage them, pressing his fingers and thumbs firmly into the arch of one.

"By everything you mean Abbie?" I looked over to where she was helping the other guys sort through the shit they'd thrown on the floor.

They did this every tour, if we stopped anywhere for long enough. Pants, shirts and socks got dropped as they hurried around doing other things. Then when it came time to pack, it all had to be picked up and claimed by whoever dropped it there in the first place.

I was pretty sure half the time it ended up belonging to someone else. No one seemed to give a crap, so it happened again and again.

Channing and I, we kept our stuff in or near our cases, most of the time. I mean, sometimes clothes went flying and you had to deal with it later.

"I know you were worried she was going to walk away from us." He started to work my toes, massaging his way up each one after the other.

I leaned back against the couch and groaned. What can I say? He had magic fingers.

"She said she won't and I believe her," I said. I tried not to pull my leg away when he touched a ticklish spot. "Do you?"

He didn't answer for a while. "I think she means it when she says that, but sometimes life happens." He pulled my foot back and started on my big toe.

"Yeah, but life could happen to any of us," I said. "What if you get an offer to play for a bigger, better band?"

He frowned. "Are you saying there's a bigger,

better band out there than Wolf Venom?" He pressed his thumbs hard into the ball of my foot.

"Not yet, but you never know who might break out." I closed my eyes. "You might decide to join Blazing Violet."

"According to Ryan, part of their job description is ducking to avoid getting hit by flying shoes." Channing grimaced. "At least around here, I only have to dodge flying insults."

I chuckled. "You might get danger pay working with them."

"Are you trying to get rid of me?" he asked lightly."

I opened my eyes a crack. "Never," I said firmly. "That is never going to change. Not ever. None of us are going anywhere. Except to America tomorrow. Just think, we can be eating New York cheesecake soon." My mouth watered at the thought of it. Was there a better food on the face of the planet?

Okay, pizza came a close second.

He didn't look as excited about that as I expected or hoped.

I sat up. "Chan? Are you okay? You keep getting this look on your face like you think someone is going to kick your puppy. I'm not walking away from you. Neither is Abbie. She cares about you as much as I do. As much as the rest of us do. You are our person." It was usually him reassuring me, not the other way around. But lately, he just seemed... Off.

"Are you having second thoughts about her? Or about sticking with the band?" Touring was exhausting at the best of times and it was easy to get sick of seeing the same faces day after day. Especially this tour when we couldn't get out even the small amount we usually did. I didn't mind being around my family all the time, even if they were occasionally dysfunctional, but I knew it could chafe the others.

"No," he said quickly. "It's nothing like that. It's just..." He wouldn't meet my eyes.

"Sweetie," I said softly, "what is it? You know you can talk to me about anything. Right?" I'd hate it if he thought there was something he couldn't tell me. No matter what it was, I wouldn't judge him. I loved him with my whole heart. He was, hands down, the best guy I knew.

"I know." He'd paused in massaging, but he started again now. "There's really nothing to say, and if there was I'd tell you. I think it's just the pressure of the tour and trying to keep being amazing night after night. Part of me thinks that we have to have an off night sooner or later. The more concerts we play, the closer we come to that night."

"You would never not be amazing," I assured him. "Besides, if we had an off night, chances are it would be because of me." Or Asher, but the drummer would roll with it so the audience never noticed. If I screwed up, I'd probably do it in a way the whole world could see.

Hard pass.

"It could be because Zeke fell off the end of the stage," Channing said. "Or the sound failed. Or the lights. Or the audience hated us for some reason. Or there's a tornado in the middle of the concert. Or a swarm of bees."

"I see you've given this a lot of thought," I said lightly. I didn't want to laugh at his fears, but the last two were kinda funny. Although, now I thought about it, they were more plausible than the rest of his suggestions.

"The audience isn't going to buy tickets to see us if they hate us," I pointed out. "The rest of it is beyond our control and they'll know that. I mean, if the sound fails we could still play. If the lighting fails, we can play in the dark." I smiled wickedly. "Or we could do something else in the dark and imagine fifty thousand people watching us do it."

He grinned in response to that. "I think you'd prefer to do that with the lights on, wouldn't you?" It wasn't exactly his thing, but he went along with it because I enjoyed it. The same way I took part in whatever he enjoyed.

"Well…" I couldn't deny it, because it was true. The one downside to being a rock star was having to maintain a certain image. Ours was far from squeaky clean, but fucking in front of that many people might be going a bit too far.

Maybe I would be a porn star in my next life.

"Are you sure that's all that's bothering you?" I asked. "Fear of failure? Or…fear of screwing up? I can't imagine anything happening that we couldn't come back from. We've done a pretty good job at dodging trouble so far. I mean, if anyone but us had found those heads…or if a camera recorded what Tully did to his adopted father… Things would have been different, but we still would have dealt with them. We have the best manager and label behind us."

Jackson in particular, had to manage some unusual things. And he did it without blinking, although not without vomiting. He'd do it again too, because he loved us. And we loved him, even though we gave him a lot of shit.

I was kinda hoping he and Abbie would hook up, because then I might get to see him naked. I'd imagined it quite a few times before. Not as often as I thought about Channing or Abbie naked, but I was only human. Jackson was kinda hot. I could easily picture him sliding his cock into Abbie, and touching her.

And yep, now my cock was getting hard. When was it not?

"I know," Channing said. "I'm just being paranoid. When the tour is over, I'll look back and laugh at how stupid I was to even think it."

"Of course you will," I said. I couldn't shake the feeling there was something else going on with him, but if he wasn't going to tell me, I wasn't going to push. All I could do was be here for him when he was ready to talk about it. And hope he did before it got the better of him.

I knew as well as anyone how bad it was to bottle things up inside. It would nibble and nibble at you until finally it took a chunk.

I'd done it too many times as a kid. I tried to avoid doing it now, if I could. Maybe if I opened up then, I would have got the help I needed. Or I would have gotten bullied.

I couldn't change the past, but I could make sure I

learned from it.

"I never knew you were worried about bees," I said lightly.

He shuddered slightly and started to work on my other foot. "They freak me out with all their buzzing and shit. Not to mention the whole 'sticking a stinger into you and then dying' thing. I mean, what's with that? People do weird stuff, but that's pretty fucking weird, don't you think?"

"I guess so," I agreed. "On the other hand, they're just doing what they have to do to protect their hive. We can both relate to that, can't we? We would do anything for these clowns." I jerked my head towards the guys. "And Abbie," I added in case Channing thought I was referring to her as a clown.

To my surprise, Channing flinched. "Yeah, there's nothing we wouldn't do for them or each other," he muttered.

There it was again, the thought that he was worried about something in particular. Something big. My heart thudded rapidly in my chest, a combination of fear and worry.

"Channing—" I started.

"We should think about ordering dinner," he interrupted. "Maybe something typically German, like sausages." He had that look on his face like he'd moved on and wanted me to do the same.

"Yeah, okay." I tried not to be whiplashed too badly at the sudden change of topic. When he was like this, there was nothing I could do but go along with it.

"And lots and lots of German beer for Asher," I added louder.

Asher looked over and grinned. "Hell yeah. Sounds like a plan to me."

Zeke rolled his eyes and threw a folded up shirt at Asher. "I thought you were never drinking again."

Asher caught the shirt and dropped it into his suitcase.

"He was always drinking again," Penn said before Asher could respond. He seemed more relaxed after his conversation with Abbie.

I'd heard them say they loved each other. That made my heart happy. When the time was right, I looked forward to saying it to her myself.

"And then," Penn continued, "he can bitch and complain on the flight over to the states. Dibs on sitting somewhere else in the plane."

"Maybe you should get drunk with him?" Tully suggested. "Then you two can have a bitch-off."

"If that happens, dibs on not sitting near either of them on the plane," Zeke said.

"The rest of us can sit up near the front," Abbie said. "Or better yet, the back, where no one can see what we get up to." She grinned wickedly.

Zeke grabbed her hand, pulled her to him and kissed her. "I like the way you think. I also like the way you fuck."

"Back at you," she told him.

I watched them kiss and his hands started to roam over her body. Things were getting hot and heavy very quickly, but in the back of my mind I was still worried about Channing.

Something was up and I had no idea what it was.

2 2

ABBIE

"Psst."

A hiss in my ear woke me up.

"Hmmm?" I blinked a few times and opened my eyes. It was still dark. The clock on the bedside table read three a.m. The only sounds were deep breathing and Asher snoring.

A dark shape crouched next to the bed.

I sucked in a gasp and sat up. I started to speak or scream or something, but a hand clamped over my mouth.

"It's okay, it's just me," Landon whispered. "I didn't mean to scare you." After a moment, he lowered his hand to my shoulder.

"What the fuck?" I whispered back. "You scared the shit out of me. What's going on?" Were we supposed to leave ridiculously early and I'd forgotten? No, I didn't think so.

"It's Channing," he said. "He got up, put on some clothes and left. He thought I was asleep but I wasn't. I was watching. I… I don't think he was sleepwalking."

It took a moment for my half asleep mind to get around what he was saying.

"Left? Where would he go?" I sat up a little more, not bothering to tug the blankets up over my bare breasts.

There was just enough light for me to see him shake his head. "I don't know. Something was bothering him, but he wouldn't tell me. I'm worried he might have gone and done something silly."

My heart stopped for a moment at the thought of what Landon was implying. When it started again, it was racing.

"How long ago did he leave?"

"Only a couple of minutes," Landon said. "I was going to wait and see if he came back, but…"

"You want to follow him," I finished for him.

"Yeah." He sniffed and I wondered if he was crying. He was definitely worried.

So was I.

"I'll come with you." I pushed off the blankets and

searched around for some clothes to pull on. That was my bra and panties, and my track pants, but someone else's T-shirt. From the smell of it, it was one of Zeke's. It was huge on me, but it would do for now.

"Should we tell Zeke?" Landon asked tentatively.

I hesitated and shoved my phone into my pocket. "Let's see if he's out in the corridor, or somewhere close by first. If we can't find him, we'll wake up the others." I hated waking people up even more than I hated being woken up.

Channing had probably gone for a walk around the hotel to get some air or help himself sleep or something. There didn't seem much point in rousing everyone for that.

"Okay," Landon agreed. He put a hand on my arm and we opened the door as silently as we could. It creaked slightly at first, loud enough to make me wince, but slid open the rest of the way without a sound.

Asher muttered in his sleep and rolled over before he went back to snoring. None of the other guys so much as moved.

We crept out and closed the door behind us.

The corridor was lit all the way along with dim lighting. It illuminated well enough to see there was no one else out here but us. Mindful of people sleeping in other rooms, we walked silently to the elevator.

"It's on the ground floor," Landon whispered. "He might have taken it down."

"Let's check if he's in the foyer," I said. I glanced back to our door, half expecting it to burst open and the other guys to come tumbling out. It didn't. It remained closed.

Landon nodded and pressed the button.

I don't think either of us breathed much while we waited for the elevator to come up to us. It felt like an hour, but it was probably two or three minutes at most. It didn't stop anywhere else.

The noise of it coming sounded like a freight train. Surely it would wake the whole hotel?

Probably not. It sounded loud because it was so ridiculously early in the morning.

The doors slid open with a whoosh and we stepped inside.

"Does he do this kind of thing often?" I asked as the doors slid shut, closing us in.

"Taking off by himself? Sometimes," Landon said. "He needs some space once in a while to do his thing. I worry I'm crowding him. I try not to be too much." He sniffed.

I turned to face him. I pressed the length of my body to his and cupped his cheeks with my hands.

"You're never too much," I said firmly. "Everyone needs time to themselves, even if it's only five or ten minutes. We'll probably get down to the foyer and find him waiting to take the elevator back up. Then we can all go back to our room and go back to bed." I kissed him lightly on the jaw.

"Yeah, I hope so," he said. "I just wish he'd told me what was going on in his head."

"He gave you no idea what it was?" I asked. I thought back over the last few days, but couldn't recall Channing saying anything worrying, or seeming upset. Although, he was difficult to read at the best of times.

Landon scrunched up his face in thought. His cheeks, just under his eyes, shone wet in the elevator light. He dashed the tears away with the back of his hand.

"He said he was scared I would leave him for you, but I told him that wasn't going to happen. I want us all to be together. I choose both of you." He wiped under his nose.

"I choose both of you too," I said. "All of you. I would never ask you to choose me over Channing." They were bringing me into their relationship, not replacing one of them with me. Still, I understood the hesitation or insecurity. This was new to all of us and we had to navigate our way through growing relationships and big feelings. Of course there would be times when we would question things. As long as we kept on communicating, we'd get through.

"I know." Landon nodded. "I guess he had a moment of insecurity. I hoped I'd put his fears to rest, but now I don't know." In a hoarse but urgent whisper, he added, "What if I never get a chance to do that? What if he decided he couldn't—"

"You will get to tell him everything you want to tell him," I said firmly. "Channing isn't going to leave you. Neither am I."

It wasn't just tears I saw in his eyes. It was also terror. The idea of being alone was almost enough to make him fracture into a thousand tiny pieces. If I had to tell him every day that I wasn't leaving, then that's what I would do. Until he understood I meant it.

Anything else he might have said was interrupted by the ping of the elevator arriving on the ground floor. It bumped lightly before coming to a stop. The doors slid open smoothly onto the low lit foyer.

I lowered my hands from his face and laced my

fingers in his. Like that, we stepped out of the elevator.

Soft music played from behind the check-in desk. Someone was on duty twenty-four hours a day, but I couldn't see them right now. Presumably they were off attending to something, or having a nap in the back and hoping no one saw them.

"He might have gone to the kitchen hoping for a snack?" I suggested.

"Right. There's always someone on duty in places like this," Landon agreed. "In case someone needs room service in the middle of the night."

Rich people problems.

Rich or not, Channing wouldn't be the first person to be hungry in the early hours of the morning. We hadn't left much of last night's dinner, between the seven of us.

"Let's go and look," I said. With any luck, someone would be taking a tray of baked goods out of the oven and we could grab some. I wasn't hungry until I had that thought. Unfortunately, none of the smells in the vicinity of the kitchen were pastry-like.

The door to the restaurant was closed but not locked. Landon pushed it open and we looked around before walking toward the kitchen.

"You hear that?" Landon tugged my hand, pulling me to a stop.

"Hear what?" I froze and listened. My mouth formed an O.

The sound of groaning and panting was coming from inside the kitchen.

"Maybe the chef is moving a side of beef?" I whispered.

"I think someone is definitely moving meat," Landon said. He looked like he was terrified one of those someones might be Channing.

If only to ease his mind that Channing wasn't cheating, I stepped over to the kitchen door and peeked inside.

That explained why the reception desk was empty. The receptionist was bent over a workbench, and the chef was pounding his meat into her. I hoped that bench would be thoroughly cleaned before any food was prepared on it. At any rate, they both looked like they were enjoying themselves. The receptionist's mouth was open and her eyes were closed in ecstasy.

Since everything seemed to be consensual, I pulled my face back before they saw me.

"No sign of Channing," I whispered. If he'd come in here for something to eat, he would have walked right past them. Even in the throes of passion, they would have noticed a buff rock star passing by. He was hard to miss.

"I'm starting to think we should go and wake up Zeke," Landon said reluctantly. "And the rest of the guys."

"Yeah, but let's go and have a look outside the front door first. He might be standing right outside, getting some air." At this point, I knew I was clutching at straws, but I didn't want to think Channing had wandered off somewhere by himself.

I mean, he was a grown man, he could do what he wanted, but I didn't want to have a box turn up outside the door in the morning with his head in it. The idea both turned my stomach and broke my heart. Of all the guys, Channing was the one I knew the least, but I didn't want to lose him.

I reminded myself Pete was dead, so Channing couldn't end up a disembodied head in a box. A tiny voice in the back of my mind reminded me that maybe it wasn't Pete who did that. Maybe it was someone else. A stalker or a crazed fan. Or someone who liked to kill people I knew and put their heads in boxes.

Shut up, I told that voice. It had to be Pete, or

there was a killer still running around, and that idea was horrifying.

"Okay," Landon agreed.

I think he would have agreed to just about anything I said right now, as long as we found Channing. His hand was hot and sweaty in mine, but I didn't let it go. That contact might be the only thing keeping him from freaking out. If that was the case, then I would hold on to him until he didn't need me to anymore.

As quietly as we could, so we didn't disturb the fucking in the kitchen, we walked back across the foyer to the front door.

The street outside the hotel was empty of cars apart from one or two parked by the side of the road.

At first, I thought it was empty of people as well. Then I saw someone walking away from the hotel. I knew that walk and the way he carried himself. What the hell?

I pushed open the door and stepped outside.

"Jackson?"

23

ABBIE

JACKSON STARTLED and spun around to face us. "Fucking hell, you scared the shit out of me." He put a hand to his chest. "What are you doing out here?"

"I was going to ask you the same thing," I said. "Are you going somewhere?"

"No. Yes." He shook his head.

"It has to be one or the other," Landon said.

"I couldn't sleep. I was sitting, looking out my window and saw Channing walk past," Jackson explained. "Where is he going?"

"That's what we wanted to know," I said. "Landon saw him leave the room." I didn't want to use the words 'crept out' in case whatever was going on was completely innocent.

"You saw which way he went?" Landon asked eagerly.

Jackson waved down the street. "In that direction." He looked from one of us to the other of us and sighed. "There's no point in telling you to go back to your room, is there? Either I let you go with me or you will follow me."

"Exactly," I said. "And we're wasting time. The longer we stand here talking about it, the further away he'll be."

"Right then, come on." Jackson turned back around and kept walking.

I exchanged glances with Landon and hurried after him.

"How did he look?" Landon asked when we caught up. "Was he upset or anything like that?"

"I couldn't tell," Jackson said. "He had his head down, hurrying down the road."

"Hurrying?" I echoed. "Why would he be hurrying?"

Where did he have to go that was so important? And why didn't he tell any of us he was going? Okay, I could answer that last bit. Zeke wouldn't have let him go. To be fair, the rest of us wouldn't have either. The thought of any of us wandering around

Frankfurt alone, in the dark, was disconcerting and fucking scary.

"For all we know, he's gone to get ice cream and was hoping to get back before anyone noticed him leave," Jackson said. "We could be worrying over absolutely nothing."

"It wouldn't be the first time he's had sugar cravings in the middle of the night," Landon said. "Since the kitchen was out, he might have decided to go looking."

When Jackson gave him a questioning look, Landon told him about the receptionist and the chef.

"Ah, I see. I wouldn't have interrupted that either." Jackson nodded. "Maybe we should look up late night strudel cafés and head there if we can't find him soon."

"I don't think they have strudel cafés, as such," I said. "Just cafés that may or may not serve strudel."

"Are you pointing that out so you can say strudel?" Landon teased lightly. He was still worried, but obviously trying to take his mind off things a little.

"Maybe," I said. "It's a cute word." Although, I was starting to get hungry for strudel now.

"Any idea what's down this way?" We only passed

a few people here and there and the occasional car zipped by.

"Hotels and a handful of restaurants," Jackson said. "The usual stuff you find in cities." He spoke lightly but he was stepping warily. Every so often, he would glance over at us like he wished we would go back to our hotel room.

Zeke was going to be pissed when he knew we'd wandered off alone. There were three of us though. We would keep an eye on each other.

"Zeke might handcuff you to him after this," Landon said. He must have sensed my thoughts.

"He can try," I said with a snort. I didn't object to the idea of Zeke handcuffing me, but not to stop me from going anywhere. Besides, it would make performing difficult and raise a bunch of eyebrows.

I glanced back towards the hotel. It wouldn't be long before one of the guys woke up and noticed we weren't there. They would wake up the rest and undoubtedly raise hell.

I pulled out my phone and put it on silent. If they tried to ring me, I would feel it vibrate, but it wouldn't wake the whole neighbourhood and scare the shit out of us. Judging by the lack of messages on the screen, the guys hadn't woken up yet.

I shoved my phone back into my pocket.

"Maybe we should try calling Channing and asking where he's going," I said.

"I did before I hurried down," Jackson said. "He didn't pick up." The potential implications of that hung in the air, but he didn't say anything more.

"His phone is probably flat," Landon said. "I'm forever reminding him to charge it. Or I take it and charge it for him. If I left it to him, it would never get done. Ironic, considering how much he loves his phone."

"Yeah, I'm sure that's it," Jackson said, sounding not at all sure.

"We'll find him soon," I said. "He wasn't that far ahead of us." He could walk faster than the slowest of us and that was me. I was shorter and had smaller legs. Long, but not as long as his. If he was hurrying like Jackson said he was, then catching up might be difficult.

For the first time, I felt bad for not suggesting Jackson and Landon go on ahead, and gone back to the hotel room. If I slowed them down and they didn't get to Channing in time...

I could be worrying for nothing. There may not be anything to get to him in time for. Nothing dire anyway. Like many things in life, it was the not knowing that was difficult.

"Only a couple of minutes," Jackson agreed. "As long as he didn't jump into a taxi or a rideshare. He could be just about anywhere if he did that."

Landon groaned. "We should tell Zeke and the others. He could be anywhere and we need us all to be looking—"

"Shhh," Jackson said. He waved us all over into the shadows of the building beside us.

I ducked in behind him and Landon slipped in behind me.

"What is it?" I whispered in Jackson's ear.

"Not what," he whispered back. "Who. I just saw the twins disappear into one of the buildings up ahead."

Sweat immediately sprung up under my arms. What were they doing here?

"Shit." I craned my neck to look around him, but saw no one.

"Fuck," Landon whispered. "If they've done anything to Channing, I'm going to rip their nuts off and shove them in their ears."

That was a new one. I had to give him credit for originality. I wasn't sure if it was physically possible but I liked it.

"I'm going to go and have a look," Jackson said.

He looked at us over his shoulder. "You're not going to stay here, are you?"

"And take the chance of you being alone with them?" I asked. "No way. Either you stay here or we all go."

Jackson muttered something that sounded like, "Who is the manager here?" but he nodded. "Fine, but stay close. I don't want to have to explain to Levi how I got you killed."

"We don't want that either," I agreed.

He started forward and Landon and I stayed right on his tail. We moved silently and kept to the shadows as much as possible.

My heart was racing so hard I was sure the twins would hear it. Surely being as evil as they were, they would have some nasty, supernatural hearing or some shit.

Okay, probably not, but it sounded loud to me anyway.

"… Really useful." The voice of one of the twins came from an open window. "Reuben sends his gratitude for all your help."

Who the hell was he talking to?

It couldn't possibly be— I couldn't even finish that thought. It made no sense at all.

"Fuck off. That's all I came here to say. I'm done."

Landon stiffened at the sound of Channing's voice.

I squeezed his hand to stop him from doing anything stupid like running into the building. If Channing was up to something, the best thing we could do stay out here and listen. What was I thinking? What the hell could Channing be up to that involved those two assholes?

There had to be something more going on here.

"Be nice," the other twin said. Parker, unless I was mistaken. "This arrangement has been mutually beneficial, remember?"

I frowned. What did that mean?

"Not anymore," Channing growled. "I don't want anything to do with you and your shit. That's what I came to tell you. I'm not gonna give you any more information about your brother or the rest of the band."

"What the hell?" Landon's voice was a harsh whisper, and a rush of hot air on my earlobe.

What the hell was right. Channing was working with the twins? Feeding them information on Zeke and the rest of us? I felt like someone stuck a knife in my chest and twisted it. I could only begin to imagine how Landon must feel.

Had Channing told them when Penn went

jogging so they knew where to find him? Had he told them about our date so they could crash it? Had he told them when I was alone both times they kidnapped me?

That thought knocked the air out of my lungs. For a solid minute, I could hardly breathe. My brain twisted and turned, jumping from one terrible conclusion to another.

"It's not that simple," Hunter said. "Remember, you're only helping us because we helped you."

What the fuck did that mean? Why would Channing help them? My heart squeezed. Had he been betraying us this whole time?

"Yeah," Parker agreed. "What do you think Reuben would do if he knew you were the one who killed Jonah?"

If I was breathless before, it was nothing to how I felt now. Landon and I both reeled and had to cling to each other to stay on our feet. I felt his ragged breathing on my neck, a caught sob suppressed so those inside the building didn't hear.

Channing did that? No, how was that even possible? Channing was...Channing. He had his moments, but he was no killer. Right?

Fuck, what if he was?

"Serves Reuben right for sending him after Zeke,"

Channing growled. "I only did what I had to do to protect the band and my brothers."

One of the twins snorted. I couldn't tell which one it was.

"Are you shitting us?" Parker asked. "You enjoyed doing it. That's why you put it in the box. So your beloved band would know what you did. It was a love letter. Classic psychotic behaviour. Right Hunter?"

"According to those documentaries you like so much, it is," Hunter agreed.

Silence fell for a few moments. "Asshole got what he deserved," Channing said finally. "And the band knew someone was looking after them. "

"How touching," Parker said sarcastically. "And we helped you to get rid of the rest of the body. How nice of us. And not just *his* body, the rest of them as well. All we asked in return was a bit of information. I don't think that's too much to ask."

The rest of them? How far did this go?

Just as I had that thought, I knew the answer.

Vance.

Poppy Newton.

Calista.

Maybe even Pete.

I don't know how it happened, but I ended up

sitting on the concrete, wrapped around Landon and Jackson, trying like hell to catch my breath while my head spun faster than a tornado.

All the people who hurt me, apart from the twins themselves, who were killed, it was never Pete, or a crazed stalker. Not a deranged fan.

It was Channing.

***

THANKS FOR READING! Saving Abbie concludes in Encore

ABOUT THE AUTHOR

Maggie Alabaster writes reverse harem and, para-normal, sci-fi and fantasy romance.

She lives in NSW, Australia with one spouse, two daughters, one dog, and countless birds.

Jo Bradley writes contemporary romance.

Sign up for my newsletter! Sign Up!

Join my reader group! Join here!

Follow me on Bookbub! Click here to follow me!

Check out my website- www.maggiealabaster.com

Book 1 Summoned by Fire

Book 2 Summoned by Fate

Book 3 Summoned by Desire

Shifter's Vault

Book 1 Discarded

Book 2 Deceived

Book 3 Disgraced

My Alien Mates

Book 1 Star Warriors

Book 2 Star Defenders

Book 3 Star Protectors

Academy of Modern Magic

Book 1 Digital Magic

Book 2 Virtual Magic

Book 3 Logical Magic

Complete Collection

Summer's Harem

Book 1: Shimmer

Book 2: Glimmer

Book 3: Flicker

Complete collection

Short reads

Taken by the Snowmen

Jingle All the Way

Also by Maggie Alabaster and Erin Yoshikawa

Caught by the Tide

Book 1–Pursued by Shadows

Book 2 Pursued by Darkness

Book 3 Pursued by Monsters